THREE INTO TEN

A SEQUEL TO THREE INTO NINE

PETER R. BRUMLIK

Archway Publishing books may be ordered through booksellers or by contacting:

Archway Publishing
1663 Liberty Drive
Bloomington, IN 47403
www.archwaypublishing.com
1 (888) 242-5904

ISBN: 978-1-4808-9306-1 (sc)
ISBN: 978-1-4808-9307-8 (e)

Library of Congress Control Number: 2020913153

Print information available on the last page.

Archway Publishing rev. date: 07/30/2020

Dedication

This book is dedicated to two comrades in arms, Col. Greg Dillon, US Army (Retired) and Col. Dana Kwist, US Army (Retired). Both of these Vietnam Veterans served their country during a time when no one uttered the words "Thank you for your service." They each continue to serve their country and do it gladly because it is their sense of duty and privilege. Each of these men could write a book of their own. This book is also dedicated to my wife, who has never failed to encourage me. Lastly, I wish to remember Audrey Hamill, a British National Health Service nurse in Norfolk, England, whose memory will always remain with me.

Acknowledgements

I am indebted to my editor Sue Dillon whose tireless efforts and dedication brought clarity and life to the prose of this book.

Preface

Much has been written about America's failed foreign policy in Southeast Asia and the tragic war in Vietnam. Vietnam has become America's albatross, and those men and women who survived the war, wear that burden daily as they try to make sense of what they had been asked to do, and how they were thanked for their service.

On the other hand, prior to the American adventure in Vietnam, the French too failed to win "the hearts and minds" of a colony that refused to obey, and in fact, were beaten mercilessly. It was inconceivable that in the twentieth century, a peasant army could vanquish military modernity. It was implausible that in 1954, the Vietnamese would claim victory over the French, culminating in the final battle of the Indochina War in the valley of Dien Bien Phu.

The story of the French Indochina War was told in my first novel *Three into Nine* as it followed three companions from very different backgrounds throughout a period of nine years. *Three into Nine* is also a tale of the French Foreign Legion, told through eyes of Sal Hecht, a young American recruit. The Legion's history, traditions, and its abandonment by the French in Indochina unfold as Sal is joined by his friends: Avram, a young Auschwitz survivor, and Jaehne, a sergeant who deserted the German Army shortly before the end of World War II.

After the final battle in May of 1954 at Dien Bien Phu, the Vietnamese captured 10,000 men, among them Legionnaires, Colonial forces, and men of the French Army. In August, after signing the Geneva

Accords that formally ended the war, the prisoners of war were repatriated to France; by then, only 3,000 remained alive. Avram and Jaehne were not among them.

Three into Ten begins where *Three into Nine* ends with the fall of Dien Bien Phu.

The history of resistance by the Vietnamese went unheeded by the French; eleven years after 1954, history would elude the United States, as well.

Peter R Brumlik
April 2020

1

Captivity

The first day in captivity was the worst, and for some, their last. The Legionnaire survivors of Dien Bien Phu, all seven thousand, dragged and forced their feet to move forward on a trail that would lead them to imprisonment. No shackles were necessary to keep them on course. There were no chains, no cages, or wire to keep them captive. Only the impenetrable jungle that engulfed them on either side prevented their escape. The green mass of foliage, vines, and razor-edged elephant grass proved to be as impassable as any barrier built to house the worst of humanity. These were French Foreign Legionnaires, however, slogging on the muddy trail. They were not among the worst. They were not criminals. They were honorable soldiers who did their duty to the best of their ability. They did the bidding of an ungrateful nation. Now, vanquished, they were on a trail leading to God knows where.

Each of the men, pushing themselves onward as if in a trance, reflected on how circumstances had placed them in what they considered to be the armpit of the world known as Indochina. This was a time when every colonial power in the world had come to accept that the era of colonialization had ended. France alone, out of obstinance and greed, had reclaimed the newly created Vietnam. France had reverted to colonialization at all costs in the region it had called French Indochina. It became the duty of the French Army and French Foreign Legion to maintain peace and order in a country that resisted both. While the French military maintained control of the major cities, the Vietnamese held power in the countryside. With that power, they acquired the loyalty of the peasants who lived there.

For nine years, guerilla actions in Vietnam took their toll on the French. The people of France grew weary of the lack of progress in a colony so far away and for the French, taking and keeping possession of it grew unimportant. The treasury of France suffered as well, since waging war was expensive and little profit from it was realized. The dissolution of the French empire was at hand.

The men of the French Army and, in particular, the French Foreign Legion, knew little of the politics behind their struggle. They were mired in battles and skirmishes that cost them dearly in lives and in equipment that would not be replaced. These soldiers had been manipulated while fighting a colonial war that was lost long before it had begun.

Laboring on the trail that had become a quagmire, most of the captive Legionnaires thought wearily about the last battle that had led them into their present circumstances. Those who no longer puzzled over their defeat and, in fact, no longer thought about anything at all, sat or fell into the mud and died. The Vietminh who guarded them suffered the same privations, fatigue, and hunger, thus abandoning the Legionnaires who fell alone. There was no prodding or abuse. The nearly dead were left alone to become the certain dead.

The valley of Dien Bien Phu had been held together by the sinews, tenacity, and will of the Foreign Legion. They had been sent there by an incompetent French Army general who preferred sacrificing the Legionnaires rather than his own men who found safety in Hanoi. The Legionnaires in the valley, were surrounded by mountains on all sides; mountains upon which the Viet Minh enemy had hauled large artillery armaments by dismantling and carrying them piece by piece, and bolt by bolt, then aiming them point blank at the garrison below. Indeed, the

Legionnaires, while believing that their tactical situation was untenable never thought that the enemy was capable of placing guns on the jagged mountains that surrounded them.

In the valley below were little forts which were no more than barricaded mounds and bunkers. These were constructed in order to prevent the ground attack that proved to be imminent. Each fort had been named after the mistresses of the incapable and vain general who remained in the relative security of his headquarters in Hanoi; far from the third circle of hell that was about to be invaded and torn apart.

After a three-month bombardment from above, the Vietminh attacked from below the ground, digging their way beneath each bunker. One by one, the little forts of Dien Bien Phu fell to the little brown people who, like ants, crawled and clawed their way over every inch of the garrison. A Vietminh force of arms that seemed unstoppable, raped outposts and bunkers, blowing each of them to bits, including the men that defended them.

'Beatrice', was the first to be blown into vapor with all of its occupants becoming a permanent feature of the valley, a mixture of blood, flesh and mud. Soon after the fall of Beatrice, each of the little bunkers fell to the Vietminh who had conquered each one by tunneling beneath them and setting charges to be detonated from a distance. The occupants of the bunkers were in horror as they heard the digging beneath their little citadel, understanding its implications and realizing that their lives were coming to horrific and speedy end. Evacuating the bunkers was futile for the Legionnaires as they would be targeted by the guns above. At the same time, they knew full well that by remaining inside meant that they would be annihilated by an enemy they could only hear. The battle was over; the conclusion was obvious.

The vanquished, no longer running at a crouch, diving for safety or defending themselves became acutely aware of their surroundings. The Legionnaires stood still, even as the enemy approached, noting the pungent smell of cordite still smoldering in the ground. They could suddenly appreciate the entire valley, verdure velvet emerald mountains, the heights from which death had rained down upon them. And, for the first time in months, there was utter silence; not even the birds that had been ever present prior to the battle were to be seen or heard. The men looked at each other, smothered with mud and, for some, their uniforms and skin stained with the blood of their comrades. They noted the upheaval of the surrounding earth that had been sculpted into a twisted and grotesque landscape of logs, sandbags, and, of course, remnants of soldiers' bodies. Some of their comrades' remains were left whole, while others in an assortment of torsos, legs and empty uniforms. And, finally, for the first time in many months, even though they would become prisoners, the Legionnaire's neck muscles could relax, and deep, full breaths could be inhaled.

Silently, without provocation, the Vietminh collected the weapons that lay on the ground in front of the overpowered soldiers. Almost politely, and only with directions given by hand-signals, the survivors were shepherded by the Vietminh to the trail upon which many were to die and the rest to languish in a prison camp.

Nine years of fighting for French Indochina ended in the valley of Dien Bien Phu. Indochina was no more. Instead, Vietnam had risen from the ashes of an unmanageable colony to a nation that had won its independence. The last glimpse of the valley that greeted the Legionnaires before they marched away was that of a flag being planted into the mound that was once Beatrice; red and blue with a yellow star in its center.

In France, after the final battle, the press held the public's attention for only one week; then, barely a mention of the land where so many of the French Army men had died. The Legionnaires were given no notice. After all, although they fought for France, they were still regarded as foreigners. Even the focus of a political solution in Geneva was hardly mentioned. The collective domestic shame of what was once French Indochina was conveniently erased from the national conscience. Appropriately, and perhaps for the best, the survivors of the disaster knew none of this. In a ragged column, the proud and honorable Legionnaires, quietly walked into oblivion.

Sal lumbered on at the rear of the column, occasionally feeling the arm of his Sergeant Major on his back as it nudged him forward. From

New York to Dien Bien Phu, Sal had journeyed; it was one hell of an adventure. The boy who had missed World War II and had wanted so badly to grow up in a uniform, got exactly what he had hoped for, except for the situation in which he now found himself. The uniform of a French Foreign Legionnaire that he wore, although in shreds, had been earned. Unencumbered by ego, jealousy, or false pretense, the camaraderie of the men he was with was legitimate. After enlisting, the most important part of his quest was recognition as a soldier who stood by his duty and being appreciated in earnest by his friends. Sadly, the imagined glory that Sal sought dissolved slowly in front of his eyes in the fifty-four days it took Dien Bien Phu to bleed to death.

The friends who had shared the great adventure with Sal had been left to rot back in the valley. Jaehne, his sergeant, the German soldier who had joined the Legion to escape an ignoble defeat of a larger European war, had been perforated beyond recognition. He had died slowly, as Avram, Sal's best friend, gently laid him on the ground and rocked him into a sleep from which he would never awaken.

Avram was no doubt the bravest of the three friends and was more of a brother to Sal than a friend. He refused a second captivity in a land so alien from his own. He refused to be interred in an Asian Auschwitz in the jungle and, by doing so, he declined a chance to live, and was shot by his captors while breaking free of the column. It was, as many of the captives witnessed, a futile attempt to gain freedom. No one could find freedom in the interwoven web of vines and trees so thick that even walls would be no more efficient in keeping the prisoners on course and on the muddy trail.

Sal, moving slowly, as if in a delirium, thought about the three of them during their short lifetime together as he made his way through the quagmire and human waste that made up the trail. This fetid, sweltering, hostile and unforgiving land is where their great adventure had come to an end. Three friendships forged out of mutual respect for each other and for the Legion unit in which they had served. Sal, Avram, and Jaehne, relegated by fate, together over a period of nine years; now, only one remained alive.

The march toward the North was as difficult for the Viets as it was for their captives. This was not to be a Bataan death march; deprivations as well as what little food existed was shared between the victors and the vanquished. The oppressive heat was not selective, and no one was immune to its power to drain one's vitality, or even one's life.

Attempts were made to revive men who had dropped from exhaustion or from the festering wounds that brought them to their knees. After the third day of struggling on the trail, it became difficult to distinguish the captors from their prisoners. The entire column became an intermingled blur of men in rags blending in with the red mud of the landscape. Maggots and lice made no distinction between winners and losers; they plagued each other's wounds equally and without reservation. Survival for all on the march depended on cooperation. The Legionnaires knew it and, more importantly, the Viets knew it, as well. The victorious had been issued orders to keep as many of their charges alive as possible because the political command thought they represented potential capital when going to the bargaining table. The tattered Legionnaires were to be pawns in an international quest for the recognition of independence by a people who, although mostly peasants, were as sophisticated as any other players on the world stage.

Escape, by even the most determined Legionnaire was unthinkable. The jungle, oppressive, impenetrable, and without light, erased any thoughts of freedom. Legionnaires knew all too well through years of fighting in Indochina that the jungle was capable of swallowing a man who ventured off the known paths. The Viets, far from becoming comrades in arms, at least extended humane courtesies toward their prisoners. Sal, who had been trained in medicine, worked side by side with Viet medics who did what they could to keep men alive with little or no medical supplies. Sal's physical strength, however, was ebbing away as the torment of men he was treating took its toll on his ability to be attentive.

Ironically, the first man to die was the battalion surgeon, Dr. Grauwin. Sal had spent countless hours with him operating on the shredded bodies of men struck down by the most accurate bombardment of guns the Viets had placed in the mountains high above the valley.

Operating by the light of a kerosene lamp in the damp bunker smelling of mold and blood, this gallant surgeon never wavered in practicing his skill while under constant fire. He neither recoiled nor stopped operating as ballistic rounds landed nearby, even when the earth trembled, and showers of dirt and debris fell over him and Sal, and sometimes into the wounds of the unfortunate one on the operating table.

Grauwin died on the trail after stumbling and falling to his knees, he looked at Sal, then dropped face forward into the mud. He died not so much from thirst or disease as from exhaustion; by this measure he should have died weeks ago. The loss of their brave and resolute doctor was an added blow to the already sagging morale of the Legionnaires. Death for him came swiftly and, compared to what lay ahead for the others on the march, he died mercifully. Sal pulled Grauwin to the edge of the trail and noticed that his doctor had left a death mask imprinted in the mud. Sal made a weary attempt to revive him, but he knew instinctively that Grauwin was dead.

As the doctor was left on the side of the trail, Sal rejoined the column without looking back. Almost immediately, he thought of René; remembering how he had practically thrown her onto the last helicopter in time to leave safely, and how fortunate she was to have escaped the valley unharmed. He remembered watching the helicopter gain altitude, tearing them apart by miles yet, knowing their hearts were forever bound by mutual love and commitment. As a nurse, René had proven herself invaluable while caring for the wounded and dying in the overburdened battalion aid station. As his lover, she would remain a part of Sal's memory forever. Sal took comfort in the knowledge that she was safe, perhaps in Hanoi, or maybe in Paris where the two of them had met. The thoughts of René brought a smile to his face as he remembered watching the helicopter disappear; a smile that soon vanished as he realized that the prospects of ever seeing her again were dismal, at best.

To put the death of Grauwin out of his mind, Sal tried to retrieve memories of the past, retracing the path that had led him to this place where he now stood. Memories flashed by with each somnolent step. There was no chronology to his thoughts, just random glimpses of the past. He thought about his hatred of New York City where he had spent an unsettled childhood; Bud, the merchant seaman who lived behind the Camel sign in Times Square, who mentored him and set him on his way to a disastrous career at sea. And, of course, Avram, his best friend, whom he met while they were both sitting on a bench in Marseilles while waiting to be inducted into the French Foreign Legion. Each frame of the silent film recollecting the past nine years was interrupted by the shadow of René. She was always there hovering over him as he knew she would be as long as he lived.

In an instant, a blunt push forward by the Sergeant Major brought Sal back to reality. He was momentarily irritated that the burly Sergeant Major interrupted his thoughts of better days, but how could Sal be annoyed by the man who had accepted and mentored him as a Legionnaire?

When it was time to eat, captors and captives sat together in a rare moment during the long hot day, exhausted, sharing what meager provisions the Viets had provided. They each ate everything and anything, above and below the ground, before the indigenous fauna of the jungle ate them. Grubs and worms once shunned as vile and unpalatable became delicacies by those who had the will and strength to eat them. Snakes, recognized by veterans of the jungle on both sides to be non-poisonous, became feasts even if eaten raw.

The wounded, regardless of which side they were on, died slowly. Pus from infected wounds integrated with tired blood as it reluctantly made its way through their bodies. Blood, once the harbinger of life, turned into the agent of death as it delivered the poison that incubated in lesions to every major organ.

Men died almost casually. Imminent death was preceded by a pattern of heralding signs. A man's plodding stride in the mud would become hesitant, then a clumsy waddling from side to side until a final stumble, dropping them to their knees, and finally, one last fall forward into the mud. There, lying prone, unable to ever stand again, the sclera of their eyes became dry and yellow, with no strength to blink and nourish them. Soon, the attempt to blink stopped and they began to stare at nothing in particular; the stare of death, unfocused, and blind to their surroundings. All human instincts to survive fled long before their hearts faded in their frail and emaciated bodies. Death became a welcome reprieve to men who no longer had the will to struggle and remain alive. Death, whether on the battlefield or as a captive in the jungle, was absolute.

The Sergeant Major, still alive in spite of his advanced age, and perhaps fortified by the years of training and discipline demanded by the Legion, slogged onward right behind Sal. Occasionally, the old mentor thrust his arms forward, giving Sal a nudge as if to ensure that he would not succumb to death's waddle. No one prohibited the prisoners from talking, but there was nothing to talk about. The monotony of the endless trail and the struggle to walk upright drained a willingness to speak; each man lost in his self-developed routine of trying to stay alive. The only words spoken were those of precaution:

"Don't drink the paddy water."

"Watch out for that guard, he's not the same as the others." "He's a Political."

The Political Officers were aggressive and the most brutal. Blowing their whistles and repeating rehearsed mantras, they swarmed the valley and demonstrated to their men with words of unyielding inspiration that the French were finished in Indochina. These squads had been infused with the ideology that led them to victory; they wielded the full measure of triumph over their non-Asian prisoners. The Political Officers had done their jobs, expressing as well as translating political dogma to conscripted peasants who knew farming and little else.

Captured Colonial troops, Algerians and Moroccans, were somewhat safer from cruelty because as men of color the Political Officers believed that the white French had used them badly and tried to influence them to realize this. Liberation, they harped, was the right for all who were oppressed. Using food as an incentive to heed their propaganda, Political Officers tried in vain to convert these men who owed their allegiance to the Legion. The Legion which had treated them without discrimination. The Colonials willingly ate the food but did not digest the ideology. They, too, realized that they would never again stand on the warm sands of Morocco or taste the sweet tea of Algeria.

After their first week on the march, one thousand men who had bravely defied the odds of losing their lives in battle were not only defeated but had also lost their will to live. Their fallen bodies, no longer noticed by their comrades, were politely stepped over with no one looking down to see whom they were leaving behind.

One thing was certain, water became the essence of life, replacing the medicine that was nonexistent. Water was a constant craving by all regardless of the uniform they wore. The equilibrium between water and sweat was shifting towards depletion by each man whose thirst became all the more obsessive. Their bodies withered. Water was the common denominator that did not discriminate between those who had won a battle from those who had lost.

Sal argued with himself as to which was worse, hunger or thirst. The small amounts of water that did exist was repugnant; one had to squeeze and sift it out of the mud that had been mixed with saliva, blood and excrement in order to obtain a drop. Some men surrendered to their thirst and, in desperation, drank of what they thought would save them. Soon, they began to quiver, then toddle, ultimately dropping into the quagmire from which they had drunk.

There was, however, water that was safe to drink for those who had absorbed the lessons of the jungle. Standing like silent stewards as the column of men filed passed them, the large leaves resembling the ears of an elephant and the vines that hung loosely from the triple canopy above held life-sustaining water. In order to take the nourishment offered by the jungle, one had to take a chance by stepping away from the column to drink from the foliage, and risk getting shot.

The Sergeant Major, however, had been well-schooled in survival because of his length of service in Indochina and knew how to drink water from the jungle foliage. Grabbing hold of vines that were within arm's reach, he pulled them down, gnawed them in half with his brittle teeth, and quickly sucked the water that was obtainable. Observant of the Sergeant Major, Sal soon learned by example and was able to drink as well.

The Political Officers held fast and were unrelenting in punishing any infraction of what they perceived was order. Using blades of elephant grass as whips, they lashed at any prisoner who was inclined to step out of line. However, because most of the other guards became as miserable as those whom they were guarding, an unspoken bond soon developed between the keepers and the kept. When the Political Officers were distracted, the guards shared their stale balls of rice with the ravenous men who were in their keep. Water was shared as well, saving many who would have succumbed sooner, until the tiniest enemy of all began the real culling of the defeated; the mosquito.

Many of the Viets had immunity to malaria and those who did not had learned to live with it. The Legionnaires were not only strangers to the land where they had fought, but also were perfect targets for the disease that spread from the mosquito. Once injected into the blood stream, the poison multiplied until finally exploding into a myriad of symptoms. Unabated fever and violent tremors were the hallmark of a disease that could humble the healthiest of men; for the debilitated, it was a death sentence. In the jungle, there was no medicine, no cure for the indiscriminate affliction that struck men down without warning. The death waddle was replaced by a tremor that led to twitching until in an anatomical progression, a violent shaking captured the chosen one. Usually, the head was the first to accede by signaling a slight nod that eventually progressed to a posture of violent protestation as if the victim were trying to say 'no' a thousand times. Then the march of symptoms caught hold of the shoulders, then the arms until the entire body had been captured in a macabre loss of control. A delirium quite different from that which the men were already experiencing took away all sense of direction, purpose, and will. Incoherent, the afflicted might as well be stumbling on the moon. The quaking sapped every ounce of energy left in these bodies already wracked by the humiliation of defeat, capture, and the sufferings of the march. Once the waves of shaking had subsided, men crumpled like deflated balloons and flopped to the ground neither awake nor asleep. Whether it was malaria, dysentery, thirst, or abject fatigue, the common denominator for the entire march was death.

Some men welcomed death as if it was the only respite from further torment. Others, too weak to fight what they could not see, defended themselves by releasing frightened tears and unintelligible mutterings until they heard a distant lullaby that would sing them to a permanent sleep. They embraced themselves with frail arms and rocked to a slow methodical tempo until they fell to their knees, then face forward into the mud and died without objection. As the march continued, the ranks of the captured began to thin by means that no soldier would have imagined.

At first, an imperceptible tremor began in Sal's lips. This was followed by the inability to focus as his head began to shake and pound. True to form, the hands and arms followed with twitching then dissolving into spasms as millions of parasites took possession of Sal's bloodstream. With each beat of his heart, a wave of heat set his body on fire, until sweat that had long ago evaporated due to dehydration was drawn from a well almost depleted. What little energy Sal had left came from an unknown resource. His breathing became shallow, then sporadic, until his eyelids fluttered, and he collapsed onto the muddy trail.

The Sergeant Major, pleading with his eyes, looked at a nearby guard for permission to attend to Sal. A curt nod allowed the Sergeant Major to drag Sal off the trail and prop him up against one of the rotting palms as the rest of the column labored by. There, embraced by one of the sergeant's arms, Sal's head gently came to rest on the big man's chest as he descended into a hallucination that would prepare him for death.

The muffled echo of laughter reverberated somewhere in Sal's head. The laughter was directed at him: an apparition of Avram and Jaehne, blurred but perceptible, were standing in front of him and looking down on his comatose body. Sal stirred, and with his eyes still closed, he leaned forward, reaching out for his friends with a trembling hand. He could see them but was unable to touch them. His friends, whose flesh had previously been shredded and torn apart, were whole and untouched by the instruments of war. Avram and Jaehne continued to laugh and point at him. The laughter stopped. Now, they were speaking to him with words that were formed, but silent, as they appeared only as vapor from their lips. Avram gestured in an attempt to get Sal to his feet as if to say, "Come join us, comrade. Leave this place and become unbroken like us. Look, we are whole and waiting for you."

The specter of Avram stretched out an arm in a slow methodical arc, almost as if he was bowing to Sal, saying,

"Come, my friend, let me take you up. Catch my arm. You can leave this place with us." Then, Jaehne joined in, hands on his hips, as if he were back on the drill field and spouted his cloud of words entreating, "Come on, you little shithead; Up you go! Get your ass moving! Listen to your old sergeant."

Sal could read their soundless words, only to hear his own desperate rasping breath. After several attempts to form words, he too could push out a cloud to talk with his friends.

"Holy shit, you fuckers are all right! You guys made it!" Each puff of his words was followed by a breath and a gurgle as his tongue searched for enough saliva to continue.

"Where the hell have you guys been? The last time I saw you was…"

"Sal, get up. Try to stand up." This time the words had a sound that did not come from his friends. It was a real guttural sound. The illusion of Avram and Jaehne was still in front of him, but the voice he heard came from a different direction. It was the Sergeant Major's voice that had penetrated Sal's mirage.

"Sal, get up, now." The order became louder, the voice replacing the vision of Avram and Jaehne, both of whom continued to laugh as they retreated into a haze until finally, disappearing altogether.

Sal partially opened his eyes searching for his friends but instead focused on a Viet guard that had replaced them. Far from smiling, the guard was threatening him by pointing his rifle with bayonet and placing it under Sal's chin. Again, the voice of the Sergeant Major erased Sal's fantasy and brought him back to the reality of his situation.

"Get up, Sal, or we're in big trouble." With one arm fending off the Viet guard and the other around Sal's waist, the Sergeant Major pulled

Sal to his feet and steadied him. Almost falling backwards towards the rotting tree, Sal swayed back and forth until the tremors slowed and he was back in the nightmare he had so willingly left behind. The welcome hallucination had disappeared. Avram and Jaehne, the two friends that had kept Sal safe, and who bonded with him in companionship during the past decisive years, would appear no more. The awareness that both of his friends were among the dead in the valley of Dien Bien Phu among hundreds of others, returned. As he steadied himself, the film of delirium cleared from Sal's head and he focused on the remaining familiar face of the Sergeant Major.

Once Sal was on his feet, he gave a nod of appreciation to the Viet guard who left with an air of contempt, but at the same time had grudgingly saved Sal's life. Guiding Sal back into the tattered formation, the senior sergeant kept close.

"You've got to keep moving, Doc. You may have some work to do; You're not finished, yet."

The old man had called Sal by the nickname given to him by the men in his regiment. He was a soldier who had gone to medical school without the traditional academic preparation, and who had proven himself not only to be competent as a combat medic but also to be courageous, as well. Above all, proficiency was paramount to qualify as a Legionnaire. Expertise in killing or, in Sal's case, healing, made a Legionnaire effective. Dr. Grauwin, the regiment's medical chief and Sal's mentor, now left behind on the trail among the rest of the dead, had left Sal in the ominous position of being the only living medical person among a column of men who were either expiring or, at some point, would die. It was this heavy burden that thrust Sal back to reality.

The rains that began as a drizzle, then came in waves and torrents urged by tropical winds, were a blessing, and a curse. Water sustained all life and revived the men who were dying from the lack of it. Men arched their faces to the sky, opening their mouths to welcome that which they had been deprived; not even the Political Officers could prevent the refreshing blessing from the heavens. The rain also cooled the men who were burning from malaria and calmed their tremors. Muscles, rigid from seizures were bathed in the cool, calming properties of rainwater. Fevers subsided albeit temporarily as the rain nourished men and infused them with a few threads of strength. Bodies that were all but spent were momentarily revived. The prisoners would need this gift of energy because the curse of monsoon rains would soon turn the trail and any paths leading to it into a muddy, swampy quagmire. It would become easier to walk without boots because the mud on the trail would suck them off their feet and indeed cling to anything that penetrated the soft, deep morass.

By the end of the first day of rain, all of the men, captives and captors, all looked the same. There was no white, no brown, no distinguishable ethnic trait; everyone was the iron-tinged color of the mud. Even the vegetation next to the trail revealed the sheer weight of the sludge, causing everything to droop or wilt. Almond-shaped eyes and rifles distinguished those who were the victors but even the Viets resembled swamp-like creatures straining to release their legs from the clumps of mud that tried to hold them fast to the earth. The Viets, realizing that haste and pushing their prisoners onward would surely kill all of them more quickly, slowed the march to a crawl; they had no choice.

After Dien Bien Phu, a new war of survival began in which the jungle and its alliance with disease, rain, and obdurate vegetation had the upper hand. The defeated Legionnaires, ragged, maimed, and ill were making their way East, and to prison.

2

Paris

Paris, in August, is hot and languid. On Sundays, the broad boulevards still wet from the morning scrubbing were seldom filled with crowds or traffic. Trees in full bloom lent shade to the few brave pedestrians who ventured out to walk their well-fed lap dogs. Very few tourists, with the exception of some West Germans, strolled by the monuments that were imperative to see when visiting the city; they had almost been destroyed during the last war.

Parisians had all but forgotten the actions that had occurred in their most recent war. In fact, France had become tired of the entire venture two years before the capitulation of Dien Bien Phu. Politicians railed against the expenditures supporting that war, debating outdated foreign policy, yet rarely mentioning the men who fought for them. France had given up on French Indochina long before the Viets had removed the prefix 'French' from its name.

In the sweltering Paris summer, Parisiennes could be seen lounging in cafés, discussing the politics of Europe as well as debating over the devaluation of the Franc; they were completely disinterested in any events unfolding in the newly named country of Vietnam, or in the men who had been sent there, and forgotten. The selective memory over the French Indochina affair demonstrated the character of the French; the nation that held liberty, fraternity, and equality as inviolable had quite simply become fickle.

Most Frenchmen had little regard or respect for the French Foreign Legion. It was a division of the French Army that, along with its parent regular army, had been sent to Indochina to do the impossible; to keep order in a colonial system, corrupt and abhorred by its native inhabitants. The Foreign Legion, vital to an army that could not function without it, historically became a continual embarrassment to the country under whose command it served. Time and again, Legionnaires did what became unreasonable for the regular French Army to do. France had an army that was mired in an archaic aristocratic chain of command that deteriorated, while Legionnaires won their battles and died bravely without notice. To the French, the Foreign Legion was expendable because their ranks were filled with non-French soldiers who had pledged an oath of loyalty to the Legion, rather than to France. Foreigners were expendable. To make matters worse, the French had little trust in the men it should have relied upon, perhaps out of ignorance regarding their service.

The French Foreign Legion developed a relationship with France that bordered on the absurd. They provided a crucial defense for a country whose army was incompetent, thereby incurring the need to rely upon foreigners to do what was known by the French as the dirty business. The French press, in particular "Le Monde," carried out a continuous character assassination in print by writing articles about Legion commanders whose only crime lay in pointing out the deficiencies of the French Army; in other words, telling the truth.

"What you do is certainly a dirty business, is it not?", one reporter had asked Colonel Cogny, the commander of the second parachute regiment. Without emotion and with complete honesty, Cogny replied, "Yes. What we do is a dirty business. But, we do it for France. If you don't want us to do the dirty business, then don't ask us to do the dirty business. Ask the French Army."

War takes a toll on those who fight it; Legionnaires were no exception.

Most individuals involved in combat, aged prematurely and often, their lives after battle became confused, deviating from a course they imagined. Faces became drawn, and battle wounds, both on the body and the mind, caused a syndrome of disorder resulting in a retreat from any ambition that had existed prior to engaging in battle. France had no patience for rehabilitating these unfortunates. As for the French Army, no such condition prevailed, for seldom, if ever, had it engaged in the furious combat with which the Legionnaires engaged on a regular basis.

This was the Paris to which René returned in 1954. Evacuated from Hanoi along with the army's high command prior to the total collapse of the colony, René, newly released from the French Army Nurse Corps, was received by a Paris ignorant of the capture of so many in Indochina who had bled for France.

Filled with melancholy and missing the man whom she loved without any doubt, René found herself returning to the only place that represented a home for her, the Descartes Hospital, where she had met and fallen in love with Sal. As she entered the reception hall, she recalled her first glimpse of him. Awkwardly probing the hospital with his steel blue eyes, Sal had looked lost as he tried to navigate the physician's register posted above the reception desk, determining where he was to report. It was his eyes that first caught René's attention, along with his short black hair; she could not resist approaching him with the intention to help him locate where he was to report.

Now, she was standing in the same reception hall, but there was no Sal. René's position at Descartes had remained vacant since she had left for Indochina, so Dr. Lebrun gladly accepted her application to return without reservation. In the familiar Descartes's operating theater, she was a welcome addition to the surgical team that knew her to be proficient and reliable. Seldom, if ever, had a staff member of this hospital ever participated in a carnage such as that of Dien Bien Phu.

René's experience as a nurse in combat did little or nothing to detract from her grace and beauty; if anything, serving as she did not only increased her expertise as a nurse but also enhanced her poise. None on the hospital staff, except for her chief, Dr. Lebrun, had been curious about where she had been or what she had accomplished. Had they bothered to ask her, René would have deferred to a polite but evasive response. Dr. Lebrun, however, held her in high esteem and knew her better than anyone, except for Sal.

The return to the Descartes Hospital by this extraordinary and beautiful woman brought new energy to the surgical residents. Those who had known her before she departed for Indochina resumed their pursuit of her. Her exquisite features also struck those who met her for the first time. René would have none of it. She was committed to Sal and determined that, at some point, they would be reunited. René knew from first-hand experience that the chances of ever seeing Sal again were slim. She had been at headquarters in Hanoi when Dien Bien Phu had collapsed. She had been in the valley and knew how horrific it had been. She witnessed the killing and destruction that occurred on a daily basis until Sal had virtually thrown her on the last helicopter to leave that place. She was present at the headquarters radio room, filled with tension as the last sputtering and fading radio transmission from the division came in. "We are surrounded. We are finished. We will not surrender, but we can no longer fight." The army staff had been puzzled by this last communication, unaware that the Legion never surrenders, but will lay down their arms and let fate take its course.

Disgusted by the cowardly actions of General Narrone, the French Army Commander in charge of all operations in Indochina, René could not understand his refusal to send a relief column to the embattled garrison. Instead, in a futile attempt to reinforce the garrison, Narrone parachuted a company of Legionnaires into the valley at night. It was, as were all of Narrone's tactics, a disaster.

Upon her return to Paris, René resigned from the French Army Nurse Corps. Her experience in Indochina convinced her that compared to the Legion, the army was ineffectual and she had nothing else to offer as a nurse. She also sensed that Parisians were apathetic and quite ignorant of the loss of so many men as a result of the war in Indochina. Perhaps, except for government officials who had washed their hand of the affair, she alone knew of the sacrifices made by the Foreign Legion.

She, along with Legionnaires, had been in hell and spit into the face of the devil. Because of Sal, she survived. Because of Sal, she kept the sweet memory of her love for him alive. She knew what kind of man he had become, how adroit he was, and the faith his comrades had in his medical skills. If Sal were still alive, he would endure. If he still lived, he would one day find a way to return to her.

As she rejected the advances of young doctors at the Descartes Hospital who hounded her, René would not let one day pass without turning her thoughts to Sal. She tried to visualize where he was and how he managed from day to day. She knew the environment in which he was trapped; She had experienced the jungle, and this made her visions of him trying to survive all the more real and horrifying.

A month after René returned to work in the hospital, the young doctors finally received her message of being unapproachable. She was perceived as the solitary Madonna; aloof, self-confident, and completely private. Her daily routine consisted of circulating in surgery, then after her shift was over, walking to the café where she and Sal had spent many pleasurable hours telling each other about their lives. With the exception of Dr. Lebrun, Sal was the only one who knew much about René's origins and life. After coffee, she would return to her little apartment on the Rue Mouffetard, the cobble-stoned lane on the Left Bank. It was a street lined with bakeries, meat and vegetable stands, and the ever-present flower market. Her apartment, too, brought back a flood of memories. There, sitting in the overstuffed sofa facing the window that looked out over the city, she and Sal continually exchanged accounts about themselves. He told her about his dislike of New York City and the journey that had led him to the Legion. René spoke about the tragic fate of her parents, nursing school, and the hospital that transformed her from a shy, provincial girl into the woman she had become. The apartment seemed isolated now and she dreamed of a day when her routine would be interrupted by the grace of love.

Occasionally, the chief of surgery, Dr. Lebrun, would take her aside and ask about her experience in Indochina. A member of the medical school faculty, it was Dr. Lebrun who had been impressed by Sal and had taken a liking to him. Dr. Lebrun fondly recalled the outsider who, without benefit of any other education or training, excelled at what other medical students had taken years of schooling to learn and process. Lebrun recalled the jealousy and rancor held by the "official" medical students, many of whom had taunted and verbally berated Sal because he had been assigned to rotate with them. "This just shows that you can train a monkey to do this job," the students had mocked.

Dr. Lebrun smiled to himself as he remembered his reply. "Yes, I suppose a monkey could do this job."

Sal, the nontraditional student, possessed an enthusiasm as well as a lack of arrogance; a rarity in the hospital that trained men of the upper classes who felt entitled to a station in life beyond the reach of mere pedestrians. Here was a young man, plucked from a military culture, and thrust into medical training for which he was unprepared. Isolated from his peers, Sal was a solitary stranger in a system that ordained education by intimidation. Sal could not and would not be intimidated, either by the medical educational process or the senior residents who fully resented his presence. Lebrun made Sal his special project and mentored him. As a result, the young Legionnaire had the advantage of being exclusively taught the curriculum he needed in order to complete his medical training. As his medical education progressed, Sal's competency, especially in the operating room, overcame any impulse by the senior surgical residents to try to frighten or divert him from his work. Over time, Dr. Lebrun developed a genuine affection for Sal and even admired the young American who had been directed by the Legion to enroll in medical school via an alternative track; a back door.

René had kept a vigilant eye on him and frequently, but silently, assisted him in refining his skills to handle the most difficult of procedures. René treasured the memory of her first meeting Sal. He, shy and hesitant in the completely unfamiliar arena of the operating room, and she, the charge nurse who would ensure that he learned his craft. She would also do her best to protect him from the haughtiness and acrimony that surrounded him.

After Sal had finished his course of instruction at the Descartes, his expertise as a medic and surgical assistant made him a valuable addition to his regiment in the Legion. His deployment and subsequent disappearance in Indochina led Dr. Lebrun to be concerned, as if the old Chief of Surgery missed him, which undeniably, he did.

Sensing that his best operating room nurse was despondent and fearing she would grow even more so when France signed the truce with the Viets, Dr. Lebrun sought to protect René as best he could. He knew that she was both private and solitary. He also knew that René would shelter and defend her emotions from intrusion. Nevertheless, his fondness for the normally reserved nurse led him to try and provide her with a safe haven.

In September, after a particularly strenuous day of operating and teaching supercilious surgical residents, who became even more so as their competence increased, Lebrun sought out René and practically had to order her to accompany him to share some wine. His choice of a café could not have been worse. They sat at the exact café and almost at the same table where René and Sal had shared a budding friendship, then later, a romance.

Dr. Lebrun ordered some wine as René sat silently opposite him, staring at her hands on her lap and contemplating the subject she knew would come up. "So, we haven't had much time to talk about your great adventure since you returned." René remained silent. The subject had been broached. "I'm sure that it was very difficult for you," Lebrun continued. "I've read the accounts of Dien Bien Phu written by Fall." Bernard Fall had been the only French correspondent to describe and give a complete account of the battle. He had been there in the valley and had managed to be evacuated just before the garrison collapsed. In fact, he had been on the same helicopter as René. In France, his depiction of the battle had created little interest among a population who had moved on to more pleasant reading.

"It was difficult," René replied, yielding nothing more as she focused on the red wine in her glass. The carafe on the table could well have been filled with blood. There was an uncomfortable silence as the man normally given to ordering all who came under his authority struggled to keep the conversation going. "You know how fond I was of Sal?" This gentle probe provoked René who took offense at the mention of Sal in the past tense. "He was quite exceptional during his training. René, you noticed that right away." Again, describing him as if he were gone forever aggravated René who, with every fiber in her soul, pleaded daily to a nameless deity for Sal's life and safe return. "He is quite extraordinary," she said. This reply caught Dr. Lebrun quite by surprise. However, when René lifted her head and looked straight at him, Lebrun was certain that he was treading on sacred ground. He decided to take a chance and probe further, perhaps to confirm what her gaze had already told him. "You are very fond of him, aren't you?" This time the mention of Sal as existing softened René's manner as her eyes flooded with tears. "Yes, I am very fond of him." The intense look in her eyes penetrated Lebrun, even touched him deeply. She was more than fond of him; she loved him. "I see. I see," Lebrun replied, as it was now his turn to lower his eyes and uncomfortably play with the stem of his glass.

René sensed kindness and concern on the part of her chief; he was after all a man she both respected and admired. At once, she gave herself permission to release some of what she had repressed and share it with him. "That valley swallowed them all up." René's unexpected introduction to the subject put Lebrun somewhat at ease. "No one came to assist them." René continued as if to relieve herself of a burden, or perhaps to share the pain she suffered daily. Dr. Lebrun, empathetic with the physical and mental anguish experienced by his patients, applied the most effective possible remedy. He listened.

"Once, at night, without giving thought to the insanity of the mission, Hanoi sent parachutists to be dropped into the valley without the aid of signal lights. They were Legionnaires, of course." René remembered the night vividly. The puffs of white billowing silk opening up against the dark sky as those men drifted to their death when they landed in the midst of the enemy. Some died horribly as they fell into the barbed wire surrounding the perimeter and became entangled. In the light of morning, one could see ghastly silhouettes of those men still in the wire, mangled, and dead. Only a few of the jumpers were fortunate enough to land within the blind drop zone.

"General Narrone was incompetent. As the commanding general, in the safety of his headquarters in Hanoi, he planned the entire failure. Of course, Legionnaires were expendable. Not once did he consider sending in his regular French Army troops." René's voice assumed an air of contempt as she recalled the General sitting in the security of his air-conditioned headquarters making grave tactical errors while looking at a map of territory about which he knew nothing. Narrone represented the divide between the French regular Army and the Legionnaires under his command.

"Sal, Avram and Jaehne were among those able to land in the drop zone unscathed." René paused as she recalled seeing Sal running at full speed dodging the random shelling that rained down upon the valley from the mountains above. Then, she recalled the battalion aid station in a bunker filled with the dying.

"In that mud bunker, Dr. Grauwin and Sal operated beneath a single kerosene lamp, dust and sand pouring down on them as shells landed above. The wounded were brought in and dropped wherever there was enough room to leave them." She described how she assisted Dr. Grauwin and Sal, desperately operating in unison, hands quickly clamping off shredded and bleeding vessels. "They worked with the speed that combat medicine requires. Unable to save arms and legs, they amputated them and dropped the useless limbs into a bucket." René remembered this in particular because it was part of her duties to empty the bucket more times that she wished to recall.

"As soon as one casualty was stabilized, perhaps losing an arm, leg, or part of his brain in the process, the next patient was placed on the improvised operating table and dissections began anew. Amidst the dust and grime, sterility was impossible. For Grauwin and Sal, the main objective was to stop hemorrhaging and keep men breathing. Treating subsequent infection was left up to the maggots that soon after surgery infested freshly dressed wounds." René could not help comparing the horrific work in that bunker with the pristine sterile conditions of the Descartes operating theater. She also pondered whether the pampered surgical residents who trained there could have survived those conditions.

"It must have been extremely difficult for the three of you." Dr. Lebrun interjected when René paused, trying to wake her from the nightmare she had just described. "Difficult?" René scoffed. Then, she was drawn back into the dream.

"Yes, it was arduous. But, Dr. Lebrun, you should have seen Sal operate. You of all people would have been proud of the skill and instinct he demonstrated. After all, you trained him."

René's eyes were filled with tears that refused to stop streaming down her cheeks as she remembered the last time she saw Sal. She described how, under the ruse of fetching supplies from the last helicopter to land in the valley, Sal had taken René with him. He placed his hands around her waist and heaved her into the aircraft at the very moment it was about to take off. There was nothing she could do. She described how she was sitting at the edge of the door being held fast by Bernard Fall, the French Journalist who covered the war. As the helicopter tilted forward to gain altitude and make its way out of the valley, René, in a uniform covered with blood and tissue, could see Sal's face as it faded in the distance.

It was late evening when the conversation between the two descended into a silent reflection. René, depleted of tears, could bear no more. Abruptly, she stood up and extended a hand to her chief. She had exhausted herself and needed to retreat. "Thank you." She was sincere. Dr. Lebrun demonstrated nothing but compassion for her. "I'm not sure how this will all turn out. In my world I can usually be certain of an outcome. But, of this I am uncertain." "I know", she replied. "But, one can hope. I must never lose hope."

"There is this, though." Lebrun wanted to leave her with something optimistic. "From what I have observed of Sal during his training, I know that he is determined, he is resourceful, and possesses strong character. Among all those attributes René, his character is most important." With the kindness of a gentleman, Dr. Lebrun gently kissed the back of her hand, instead of shaking it.

As he turned to leave, he stopped and faced her. He did not want to leave her despairing. "You, too, have character, René. I truly believe that you and Sal will be reunited one day." With that, he turned and walked away slowly, hoping that she could endure whatever lay ahead.

René's eyes remained fixed on the back of the old man until he disappeared. Worn out, she slowly made her way back to her apartment. On the way, she reflected on her conversation with Dr. Lebrun, particularly on his parting words to her. In the harsh and disciplined world of medical education, Dr. Lebrun was, after all, a very kind man.

At age thirty, René had been Lebrun's anchor in the operating room. Although a nurse, and not a physician, she supervised the surgical residents as a shepherd would guide a herd of sheep. She ensured that they would not succumb to error and, most importantly, that the patients under their care would not come to harm. When René had left for Indochina, Lebrun was hard pressed to find a replacement as diligent as she; in fact, he could not. No one had the kindness, patience, or skill that she consistently demonstrated. When she returned, Dr. Lebrun was overjoyed; immediately reinstating her to her charge nurse position.

Exhausted, René sat on her couch. She closed her eyes but could not rest. Outside on the Rue Mouffetard, the cobblestones still warm from a sun that had retired, she could hear people strolling by her window completely unaware that thousands of miles away, there were as many men, having fought for France, slowly dying in agony.

Before she drifted off to sleep, René wanted to recall something pleasing to ward off the loneliness she was sure to feel. Desperately, she summoned the memory of Sal, their first forays into friendship and, finally, their time together as lovers. They had left France as acquaintances, then became lovers in a most hostile and dangerous land.

Their intimacy was born in the little hospital of Quang Tri, amidst the tropical heat and in a rare moment of peace. She recalled that the first time they had made love was not given to unrestrained passion. Instead, she and Sal paused during each ritual that would bond them for life. After disrobing, they took time to gaze at the beauty of one another's bodies: his, tanned and solid from months of physically demanding duty, and hers, white with the texture of satin. The scattered rays of sunlight were filtered by the bamboo slats that served as a window, highlighting each curve of René's body. They found themselves in a wonderland that neither had ever imagined. René remembered how self-confident she had felt and, without any reservation, led Sal to her bed that was barely cooled by a slowly rotating fan above. They had touched in increments, each in turn exploring the body of the other with wonder and encouragement. Sal had hesitated as she invited him to lie on top of her, finally yielding as she embraced him with her arms and finally her legs. They submerged their bodies into each other as if they had received a sacrament.

Her final recollection of their first sensual introduction to one another in Quang Tri was of the peace and wonder that they had both felt as they quietly lay next to each other in an embrace, unwilling to disengage from a state of grace.

As sleep claimed her, she tried to pray. She had long forgotten the ritual but made a desperate attempt by asking whatever higher power there was to watch over Sal wherever he might be. If, he was still alive. "He *must* be alive," René quietly pleading, "Please, keep him out of harm's way." With that, René drifted off with some measure of peace.

3

The Dying

The hospital at Cao Bang near the Chinese Border was nothing like the one where Quinn had trained in Paris. The Vietnamese doctor, who had been trained by the French at the Descartes Medical School, worked feverishly to prepare for an onslaught of patients that were on their way to his understaffed facility. Although the French had trained him, his allegiance to his native country and its independence never wavered. He used his profession for the cause of liberation from the very people who had reluctantly educated him.

Quinn had heard about the great victory at Dien Bien Phu but was not aware of the scope or number of injured that were heading his way; neither did he know that French Legionnaires were among them. All he knew was that his country, at last, was free from Colonial rule and that his great leader, "Uncle Ho", had declared independence. The price for independence, however, was receiving a flood of victims who had fought on both sides and were slowly making their way to Cao Bang.

The hospital had no corridors, no sterile facilities, or wards with rows of beds. Instead, the Vietnamese medical unit was similar to all such unsophisticated hospitals in the jungle. In fact, the hospital was nothing more than a series of huts covered with palm leaves shading a hard-packed clay floor. Instead of beds, woven tatami mats would serve as a resting place for the wounded and dying men. The operating table was nothing more than a wooden platform perforated with holes in order to drain blood into sand-filled boxes placed beneath it. Kerosene lanterns provided barely enough light necessary for a surgeon to operate.

Quinn was accustomed to the primitive conditions in which he would have to care for patients at Cao Bang. For a while, he had been the chief medical officer at Dien Bien Phu. There, high above the valley, in a cave used as a hospital, he had seen the carnage wrought on humans by weapons of war. With little or no medical supplies, least of all anesthesia, Quinn had done his best to repair the wounded in order to send those who were still able to fight back into the valley. The victims who died under his care were recorded and buried on the slope of the mountains without the comfort of grave markers, suffering the additional indignity of disappearing from a people that worshiped its ancestors. Some of the casualties were Legionnaires who had been parachuted into the valley during the night and landed among the Vietminh. For these unfortunates, Quinn had been given orders to provide them with very little in the way of treatment; the dead Legionnaires were buried side by side with their enemies in unmarked graves that would decompose as the jungle claimed everything within its grasp.

Days before the French laid down their arms, when the outcome of the battle was all but assured, Quinn was ordered to make his way north to Cao Bang to await the arrival of his wounded victorious comrades. He was completely unaware that among them would be thousands of the enemy Legionnaires.

The mist surrounding Cao Bang was a mixture of charcoal fires used to boil rice and the evaporation of rotting jungle vegetation. Occasionally, a breeze would sweep down from the Chinese border a few kilometers away to the north and clear the air. During a lifting of the haze, as Quinn was making an inventory of his medical supplies, he chanced to look towards the trail leading to his hospital. At first, he saw the faint outline of what appeared to be ghosts, only to realize that the apparition was the column that had finally reached its destination. He was stunned to see thousands of men lumbering toward him, worn out by disease, and hampered by the long journey. Many men, some appearing more dead than alive, had been reduced to skeletons and were being dragged by their comrades until they reached the yard in front of the hospital. Four of the captives, upon smelling boiling rice, tried in vain to step out of the column but were restrained by the guards; their ravenous hunger would not be satisfied until the Viets had appeased their own. The guards, upon seeing the kettles of rice, soon abandoned their charges and ran to eat their ration.

Quinn, who was familiar with mass casualties, could not believe the number of victims that kept pouring into his hospital. Immediately, he knew that his supplies were insufficient to handle what was about to descend upon him; he was also concerned about the shortage of trained staff that could assist him.

Once the yard had been filled with the wounded, the rest of the prisoners sat down en masse on the trail unsure of what to do, or where to proceed. Hollowed eyes gaped at the solitary astonished doctor as he walked among them trying to assess his situation. What few orderlies and nurses there were came to Quinn's side as he walked among the sea of men, surveying the scene with dismay, and the knowledge that most of these severely wounded wretches would die. As if a curtain descended upon the multitude of men in whose midst Quinn stood, the mist that continually shrouded the camp fell. The doctor shook his head in despair as he returned to the hospital knowing that he was being confronted with a catastrophe.

Quinn ordered his senior nurses and orderlies to wander through the assembled crowd and select those most likely to live, and those who would be left on the trail to die. The starving men were weak and disoriented. Rather than giving them hope, the smell of food made them retch, spewing out the remaining bile left inside of them. These men would certainly be omitted from treatment.

As instructed, Quinn's medical staff waded through the survivors, unsympathetic, sometimes only determining a victim's survivability by the vacant stare in their eyes; those with fixed and dilated pupils were left to remain in what was to become their tomb. Realizing that selection was taking place, some of the soldiers raised their arms towards the nurse or orderly as they passed, beckoning them to pay attention to their signs of life.

The onslaught of patients was overwhelming. Quinn quickly realized that temporary shelters would have to be built in order to house them. He ordered some of the guards, who were also weakened, to fabricate palm shelters in order to get those men who might have a chance of being saved into the shade. The guards were defiant and hesitated; Quinn, however, exercised his authority as an officer. "These wretches aren't going anywhere. Do you think they are capable of escape? Look at them. They are barely alive. Some will perish by the time you finish the shelters. Now, get going!"

The culling of the patients had begun. Those who were salvageable were dragged through the slime and human waste of those who were about to die. It took most of the day to place those victims who might live into a place of shade; that act alone provided the one beneficial treatment that was immediately available. By late afternoon, as the monsoon rains began to fall, the trail leading to the hospital resembled a graveyard waiting to be covered by earth. Viet reinforcements arrived, digging ditches into which the unnamed, unrecognizable, lifeless Legionnaires would be tossed into obscurity.

The newly arrived Viet soldiers were not as kindly disposed to the surviving enemy as those who had captured them; They had not witnessed the gallantry of the men now in their keeping. Proud, and infused with the glory of independence that had been declared by Ho Chi Minh, they saw no reason to show any sense of humanity to the westerners who had nearly bled their country to death.

Quinn was powerless to stop the random beating of his patients by the new guards. The victims had not the strength to evade the bamboo rods that flailed them as they lay beneath the palm shelters. The patients may have evaded the dangers of the sun but could not be spared from the rod.

The arrival of fresh troops also brought needed medical supplies, most of which were intended to treat the victorious soldiers, also in weakened condition. Quinn had to make some difficult decisions: Who was to get the benefit of treatment, and who was not? The choice was made for him by the newly arrived Viet commander who immediately insisted that prisoners were to be left in the hands of their God; only the brave liberators of their country would receive treatment or be treated.

Quinn surveyed the scene of dying and decaying flesh that lay before him. Emaciated, weak from malaria, dysentery, and gangrenous wounds, many, if not all the French patients would surely die if left untreated. His orders were to reserve that which would preserve life for his own people. Why, then, had the prisoners been brought here? The orders from the new commander violated Quinn's principles as a physician, but he had no other choice. Overcome by the task he faced, Quinn retreated to his hut, and waited for triage to be completed.

The brief memory of his days of training in Paris overwhelmed his train of thought. He recalled being a medical student at the Descartes in Paris. He had never been treated as an equal by the French or thought of as anything other than an anomaly by his fellow medical students and professors.

Once, when casually making his way to the anatomy laboratory, he was chided by an orderly. "Why are you dallying?" Quinn looked back in surprise at the orderly who was rushing towards him. "Yes, I'm talking to you. Where are your cleaning supplies?" Perhaps, Quinn thought, he had dropped something, and that this young man was bringing it to his attention. What the orderly brought was the full force of contempt and disdain he had for the Vietnamese. "Where is your mop and bucket? Do you think you can just stroll around the halls without working? You're not back in some squalid village, you know?" Quinn replied, with his usual naivete.

"I'm a medical student here." "Impossible," the orderly replied incredulously. "How can someone like you have the brains to be a student of any sort?" Even the intervention by one of Quinn's professors did not stop the abuse. "Charles. He *is* a student." Then, after a pause,

"Unfortunately, we have to train these people in order to make them useful, then send them back to where they came from." "Unbelievable!" The word from the orderly almost spat out of his mouth as he went about his business. "We train shit like this?" "Unbelievable."

Quinn was neither astonished, nor offended. From the moment he arrived at the Descartes Medical School, he had been despised by the other students as well as isolated as an aboriginal exception. The school that was dedicated to the healing arts was itself ill. He had been condemned to make his own way through the difficulty of his studies without the benefit of peers or the customary student life.

The Colonial administrators of French Indochina were not only bleeding natural resources from the country, they were also culling intellectual possessions from a land they neither respected nor supervised responsibly. For the French, Indochina was a landmass to be drained of all that was of value, including those who had the potential to serve their own people. An uninspired administrator had selected Quinn to be sent to medical school in France after he had shown a capacity and aptitude to compete in European academia.

Quinn left for France thinking that he had been selected because of his ability; in fact, the French had deported him in order to keep a docile population ignorant and devoid of any possible leadership that might prove problematic. Quinn was apolitical and perceived himself only to be a scholar. At the Descartes, the only comfort and safe haven for the shunned Vietnamese medical student came in the form of a Legionnaire. The young man with whom he shared his quarters was also seen as a misfit: An American, named Sal.

He had been sent to the Descartes by the Foreign Legion and thrust into an academic discipline for which he had little knowledge, experience, or preparation. Sal occupied the same status as Quinn: an outsider or worse, a trespasser, in a profession that was ruled by arrogance and class distinction. Quinn, as a Vietnamese, was shunned because of his ethnicity, whereas Sal was rejected because he was a Legionnaire and an unschooled foreigner for whom the traditional pre-medical education had been waived. Alternately called mercenaries, savages or barbarians, Legionnaires were involved in doing France's *dirty business*.

Sal, the Legionnaire, shared the same living quarters with Quinn, his misfit counterpart. Over the course of their medical training, the two had become fast friends. They shared their meals, their studies, and loneliness. Sal, the more gregarious of the two, became very protective of his Vietnamese friend and did not hesitate to defend him from the daily abuse and insults hurled at Quinn by the "official" medical students. This placed Sal at an additional disadvantage because, as a Caucasian, he was perceived as turning his back on his own race. It was ironic that post-war France, having witnessed racial persecution at the hand of the Germans, now practiced the same ethnic bias.

Quinn observed and appreciated the way Sal dealt with snobbery and class discrimination; he was subjected to it, as well. Above all, Quinn resolved to accept everything the French had to offer, even their contempt, without resistance. He did not hate the French; instead, he absorbed his medical education and decided to patiently wait for the time when he could return to his hemorrhaging country and heal those whom the French had made ill; He was a very patient man.

The stench of the dying and the moans of those being beaten brought Quinn back to the reality of his situation as well as the nightmare he faced. Newly arrived coolies, who had undermined the forts at Dien Bien Phu, solved the problem of disposing of the dead. The diggers, while not bearing weapons, had been indispensable in defeating their enemy. In that valley they had scurried around like ants beneath the earth, scooping out dirt with baskets until finally reaching their destination beneath the forts, where they placed charges of dynamite. When their assault comrades were in position, fuses were lit, and the earth erupted from below. The coolies did from below, what no plane could do from above.

Now, once again, the coolies worked the earth, this time from the surface. Instead of digging tunnels, they prepared a giant crematorium for those who had outlived the battle of Dien Bien Phu but had not survived the march to Cao Bang. Legionnaires who were still able to stand were forced to drag their dead comrades and push them into the trenches. The corpses were soaked with gasoline and a match was struck.

Fire, smoke, and finally, the ashes that gently floated onto the jungle marked a thousand graves of men who had been sent to a mysterious land and had disappeared anonymously into its bowels.

The fire pits burned for three days and nights, the jungle and its red earth turning to snow as the ashes continually rained down upon it. The fetid smell of the dead from the pits wafted into the little huts where the French wounded lay unattended, slowly dying waiting for their turn to be added to the smoldering furnace. By the end of the third night, only three thousand of the original ten thousand captured Legionnaires and their Colonial counterparts were still alive.

Quinn was certain that if the beatings did not stop, what remained of the survivors, now his patients, would soon be added to the pyre. His problem, however, was how to approach the Political Officers who were certain to accuse him of anti-revolutionary sentiments if he appeared to be protective of the enemy.

What would save some of the captured were events that transpired thousands of miles away in a country devoid of jungle, in a city known for international diplomacy: Geneva.

France, its allies and Vietnam would sign the "Geneva Accords" that would set the conditions of surrender, including a disposition on what to do with the captured; they were to be repatriated, as soon as possible. The Accords also insured the dissolution of Colonialism in Southeast Asia. However, due to the interests of the United States and China, and without opposition from the French, the country of Vietnam was sliced into two sections, in a diplomatic game of chess. As a result, the death of French Indochina gave rise to the birth of North and South Vietnam: one country torn apart with the stroke of a pen.

Although Quinn was not aware of the Geneva agreement, the Political Officers were determined to exact as much punishment on the prisoners as they could until they were forced to repatriate them. To this end, the orders they gave to Quinn were ambiguous.

"You must save as many of these men as possible," they told him.

"Even though they are instruments of the French, you must do your best to save them." The order was hollow.

"I will need medicine and supplies in order to help these men," Quinn explained to the Political Officers who stoically refused to acknowledge the request. "We will provide to you what is necessary after you take care of our own comrades." They emphasized this order to ensure that Quinn received their message. He was a Vietnamese doctor, but it was well-known that he had been trained by the French. This made him suspect for harboring Western sympathies by a regime that cast doubt on anyone who had been in touch with a foreign influence. Quinn understood this and knew that his hands were tied. He knew that no additional medical supplies would be provided. The doctor was tasked to do the impossible; protest would be futile and, perhaps, dangerous. The fate of the prisoners had been conveniently placed in his lap.

"With all due respect, Comrade Commandant. I need medical supplies for all the wounded or else they will all die, including our men."

The Political Officer pondered Quinn's request with suspicion. However, he was also aware of the surrender agreement, particularly the provision that all of the captured and wounded would be given humane treatment and returned to France; fortunately, he was not aware that France had all but forgotten about the prisoners.

"How many wounded French soldiers do you have?" The officer asked sternly.

"Of the seriously wounded, fifteen hundred. The rest are ill with malaria and dysentery, but need treatment, or they will die. The ones with minor wounds have become infected and I fear that many of those patients will lose their limbs." "It was pointless for them to have been sent here in the first place." Flushed with victory but very well aware that the party-political bureau in Hanoi would hold him accountable for considerable deaths, the Officer made a concession. "I will see to it that you receive as much as we can spare, but I warn you, our people come first. Do you have any comrades that can assist you?"

"I only have nurses and orderlies. No doctors." Quinn was somewhat relieved that he would get something in materiel support but dismayed that he did not have the professional help he really needed to assist him.

"Survey the prisoners and see if there are any medical personnel among them. If there are, make use of them." With a curt about-face, the officer strode off, yelling to his subordinates to fetch whatever medical supplies there were and to bring them to the overburdened hospital.

Quinn and two of his nurses began to sift through the wounded, searching for anyone with medical training and physically able to assist them. Each hut was quiet except for an occasional moan from men who were lying on the dirt floor or, if lucky, a torn woven palm mat. Most of the casualties were severely dehydrated and seemed to be on the brink of death. Those with enough energy to sit up leaned against bamboo supports, staring without seeing, and barely taking notice of the two nurses that scurried from patient to patient asking in broken French who among them had medical experience.

"You medic? You doctor?" Using pantomime gestures animating the giving of injections or taking a pulse, the nurses found no one. They reported to Quinn by shaking their heads, then were sent off to inventory what supplies had been received.

Several of the huts had been sequestered for patients with malaria who had not been wounded. In spite of their shivering and tremors, perhaps these men were still viable. The occasional rains that fell cooled the air but in the malaria huts, the fevers and sweat that accompanied the disease turned the air into putrid clouds of condensation. Dysentery among the malaria patients complicated their condition even more. The orderlies were reluctant to enter the malaria huts because they were repulsed by the odor inside them as well as fearing a contagion. "You search the huts of the wounded," Quinn told the orderlies. "I will check the malaria huts."

As Quinn entered the first hut, the foul air that permeated the place made it difficult to inspect without gagging. He pulled off one of the palms from the shelter's roof and used it as a fan. As he came to each patient, he waved away the flies and questioned each man whether they had any medical training in fluent French. "Monsieur, avez vous l'éducation médicale?"

Generally, the response was non-verbal, such as a weak shake of the head. A few had their eyes open, but did not respond; their pupils fixed, Quinn would check for a pulse and confirm them to be dead. In one hut, Quinn was met by a patient, delirious and arching his back, with only enough strength to whisper, "Oh, please. Pour water on me. Please...let me die."

Before the doctor could ask his question, the patient's plea was answered as he slowly lowered his spine to the floor, let out a gurgled sigh, and died. The scene remained unchanged from hut to hut, until Quinn became discouraged, fatigued, and often paused to vomit before forcing himself to continue.

As Quinn entered the last hut, his eyes were immediately drawn to a large man leaning against a support pole, cradling one of his unconscious comrades. The Vietnamese doctor approached the two men, fanned away some flies, and asked his question. "Monsieur, avez vous l'éducation médicale?".

There was no response. Quinn inspected the larger of the two. Taking a pulse, he found the wrist to be ridged and cool. The large man was obviously dead. He then inspected the patient who was held fast in his arms. This young patient was still alive, though breathing in shallow gasps. His facial features were parched, distorted by skin that was drawn to his cheekbones. His eyes were closed but the thread of a pulse was still clinging to life. "Monsieur. Can you hear me?" "Peux-vous m'entendre?"

His question was answered by a murmur forced through dry, cracked lips. Quinn asked him if he could open his eyes. "Monsieur, pouvez-vous ouvrir les yeux?"

Sal's eyelids fluttered as if trying to gather enough strength to lift them open. Still in the grasp of the dead Sergeant Major, Sal slowly turned his head toward the voice that was urging him to wake. Sal opened one eye; the other remaining closed. Quinn fanned him rapidly as if trying to ward off a ghost that was about to take this young victim away.

"Monsieur. Avez vous l'éducation médicale?"

Quinn, now almost pleading with the frail patient, intuitively felt that there was something about this young man that evoked a memory from the past. Through stiff, fissured lips, Sal gave a weak reply that would ultimately save his life.

"Descartes… Medical…School."

4

Quinn

The village of Quang Tri in 1939 was a quiet paradise in central Indochina. The hamlet was a much-desired assignment for many in the French Colonial Administration. Close to the port of Tourane, the much smaller village of Quang Tri had none of the traditional French architectural influences that deprived the Vietnamese of their cultural heritage as it did in the larger cities. Hanoi, Saigon, and Tourane displayed broad boulevards that imitated the streets of Paris. Quang Tri, on the other hand, remained a small Vietnamese island afloat in a sea of French design.

The small streets, most unpaved, were lined by borders of closely planted palm trees on each side, giving shade to the small shops along the road. Tea stands and open-air vegetable vendors were busy in the late afternoon when the villagers leisurely shopped for their evening meal. During the monsoon season, the entire province would flood; a welcome source of water for rice paddies but made for a tortuous route and hinderance to vehicles that tried to make their way. The simplicity and isolation of Quang Tri revealed none of the tensions forced upon the Vietnamese by the French Colonial system. One exception was the constant shortage of rice that plagued the entire country. Much of the rice that was produced in the country would be exported by the French and sold in Europe. On the whole, however, Colonial Administrators appreciated both the charm and gentility of the location and vied for an assignment to the village.

Jacques Stein, the current administrator and governor of Quang Tri Province, had been chosen for the post, not because of his excellent administrative skills, but rather, because he was a Jew. As a Jew and the focus of traditional French antisemitism, Stein was relegated to Quang Tri in order to keep him out of the ordinary scheme of Colonial politics. French Jews were citizens of France but historically perceived by the French to be less than "French." To the French, Jews, because of their professional skills, were a necessary inconvenience.

Quinn, at the age of fifteen, had experienced very little of the hegemony by the Colonial power that plagued both his country and, more so, its people. To be certain, being a peasant in Indochina was a severe curse, more so under French rule than it had been during the intermittent Chinese invasions. Peasants who remained isolated could, however, evade some of the deprivations suffered by those in the larger cities. As a result of the numerous invasions by the Chinese, the cultural and religious life of the Vietnamese peasant in the countryside had been heavily influenced by their quarrelsome neighbor.

Quinn's family had predestined him to be a scholar and raised him in a tradition brought to Vietnam by the Chinese; the Confucian model of scholarship.

Notwithstanding numerous attempts by Catholic missionaries to convert the Vietnamese, the Jesuits competed with Buddhism, and lost. In silent resistance to the French, who had imported Catholicism along with its Jesuits, Confucianism remained embedded in the spirit and nature of the Vietnamese; Quinn's household was no exception. Rigid, and based on the principle of merit gained by scholarship, Confucianism allowed for diligent peasants to advance to a higher station and occupation by studying for various positions in the Empire.

Living under French rule, the Vietnamese peasant yearned for an afterlife in which he would be reincarnated, living freely in a state of perfection, and escaping the toil of the present.

Quinn became a Buddhist monk at age thirteen; then, much to his parent's satisfaction, pursued the Confucian path of scholarship at the age of fifteen. He was slight in stature and very shy by nature, demonstrating none of the rebellious condescension of his Vietnamese peers. His only imperfections were the pockmarks on his cheeks left by an illness that few survived without benefit of treatment; Quinn not only survived, he thrived, despite being fraught by the relentless fevers and carbuncles that blemished his face. Thus disfigured, his family was unable to make a match of marriage for him, but instead, insisted that he try to escape his position in life by studying.

Quinn's affable nature coupled with a dedication to discipline instilled in him a determination and talent for study. Subsequently, Quinn received an endorsement from his primary school master; he was then eligible to be interviewed and assessed with respect to his eligibility for further education under the tutelage of the French Colonial educational system. Should he be chosen, he would be evaluated and placed for matriculation into a field that was necessary to protect and further serve the needs of French Indochina.

Quinn was one of three students selected. This made him a prime target for recruitment by Jacques Stein, the French Colonial Administrator of Quang Tri Province as a candidate for training. Once selected by Stein to sit for the examination, Quinn became one of the few to do so. As a candidate, however, he also became suspect by his Vietnamese peers who would one day rise up and liberate their country from the French stranglehold that had choked them for more than one hundred years.

Stein scheduled Quinn's interview on Tet, the Vietnamese holiday celebrating the Lunar New Year; a good omen for Quinn. It was not uncommon to schedule official functions on Vietnamese feast days because the Colonial Administration intentionally wanted to disrupt the traditional way of life of the people they governed. In a similar way, once colonization had been consolidated, the name 'Vietnam' never appeared on maps. Instead, in order to promote disunity, the country was divided into three regions: Tonkin in the North, Annam in the center, and Cochin China in the South. This intentional derangement by the French had exactly the opposite effect. The Vietnamese saw precisely through the ruse and were secretly determined to strive for the unification of their country by driving out the French. It was just a matter of time and choosing the right moment. Patience, also a component of Confucianism, became the primary weapon for a people who had been dominated by invasion and occupation throughout their history.

Jacques Stein had many qualities that were abhorred by his superiors. Aside from being Jewish, Stein revealed that he had a passionate desire to respect the customs and traditions of the Vietnamese people; in other words, his superiors thought he had gone "native." From the moment he arrived in Vietnam, Stein began to see the beauty of not only the land but also its people. He had an affinity for Vietnamese culture and society. In no time at all after his arrival, he saw that occupation by his countrymen was a deliberate attempt to deprive the Vietnamese of their identity, as well as their land. He saw his government misappropriate rice, the lifeline of Indochina, as well as its indigenous spices for which the Europeans had developed a taste for appetizing cuisine.

Minerals, and above all, rubber, were the export prizes of the colony. Rubber trees were a special target for the Michelin consortium. Tires were manufactured from the elastic sap harvested by Vietnamese who were treated as little more than slaves. All Vietnamese goods went to France and virtually nothing was given in return. Even the promising students that were sent to France to be educated returned to Indochina to serve those who had cultivated them.

It was for this purpose that Quinn was to be interviewed. If successful, he would be transformed into a pawn placed on a French chessboard in a game whose outcome had been predetermined.

The interview took place in the Provincial Governor's mansion, quite out of place in the otherwise untouched architecture of the village. Even the palms surrounding the grand house had been foolishly cut down in an attempt to forge the landscape; all the while, relinquishing shade in its stead. Everything and everyone in that building suffered from the heat that would have been naturally kept at bay had the foliage been left in its natural state and not been tampered with. If Stein had been given a choice, he would have lived in a dwelling similar to those of the Vietnamese; a traditional house designed to withstand the fluctuations of weather brought to the land by the South China Sea.

The great white, colonial structure, out of place as it was, did serve the purpose of appearing to impose the will of a foreign power on a people who had no choice but to answer any summons originating from its chambers.

The primary school master and his three students, including Quinn, entered a spectacular central hall within the Governor's mansion to which they had been called for their examination. Prior to being escorted into the grand hall, the four of them stood patiently with their heads bowed as a sign of respect and obedience. Four ceiling fans, the blades of which were ironically shaped like the palms that had once completely surrounded and provided shade to the building, neither cooled nor circulated the stifling air. The temperature was oppressive, even for the Vietnamese who typically did not perspire.

There, behind an ornate desk, sat Stein in the only chair in the hall. He was dressed in a white suit that was drenched with sweat. Constantly dabbing at his face with a handkerchief, the repetitive motion seemed to exert an extreme effort for the Provincial Administrator; he would have preferred to conduct the interviews in one of the cooler, shaded cafés of Quang Tri, but the Colonial protocols insisted that all government business be conducted in the formal hall.

Standing next to Stein was a Vietnamese male secretary who several years prior had endured the same ritual as these three boys were about to undergo. He had been selected to learn the language of governance in order to serve as a clerk and translator. Fully devoted to Stein because this Administrator was quite different from his predecessors, the secretary would interpret as well as advise him on the answers the students gave to his questions.

The secretary opened the proceedings. "His excellency, the Governor has received the recommendations from your headmaster and wishes to ask each one of you some questions." The boys were dressed in their finest white smocks that hung loosely about their bodies, concealing any signs of trembling they each felt.

As Stein spoke, the secretary translated. "Are you each prepared to leave your families should you be selected to study in France?" The boys were either too afraid or uncertain as to whom they should reply. They nervously began to shift their feet from side to side as they continued to avert their eyes from the Governor. Stein, who was not only acquainted with Vietnamese customs but also spoke their language realized that these were, after all, children. In an attempt to put the boys at ease, he spoke to them directly and in their own language. Their reaction was immediate. Raising their heads in astonishment, they dared to reveal a hint of a smile as they looked at Stein directly.

"Don't be afraid," Stein urged in a kind and steady tone. "No one here means you any harm. I merely want to know how devoted you are to your studies."

Never before had they heard anyone who held sway over them speak Vietnamese. This Frenchman who was speaking in their own native tongue may have impressed the boys and their headmaster but aggravated the secretary who felt his position had been subverted. Again, breaking with the formality of his position, Stein reached out and grasped the arm of his secretary in order to calm and persuade him to soften his approach.

Addressing the headmaster, Stein continued. "You have my permission to speak freely, headmaster. You know these boys and their abilities well."

The headmaster bowed deeply, not only as a sign of respect, but also as a token of appreciation for being addressed in his own language.

"Monsieur Governor, I present these boys to you because they have shown themselves to be truly dedicated to their lessons. They have all passed my examinations. I believe that they all have merit."

Stein, sitting uncomfortably in the sweltering room, stood up, circled the table, and leaned back on it. He looked at each boy, nodded his approval, then began to question each one individually.

"You, Boy." Stein pointed to the first in line. "Tell me about your studies."

The headmaster walked behind the boy and gave him a nudge forward.

"I am a student of history," the boy answered speaking more to the floor than to Stein.

"Ohh. I like that subject. What kind of history?"

Again, a nudge from the headmaster prompted a reply.

"The history of Vietnam, your excellency." The secretary shot him a look of disapproval; he should have replied French Indochina.

"Are you aware of the king known as Le Loi?" Stein asked, a remarkable question coming from a French administrator. As a rule, none of them knew anything about the history of the country they ruled. But, Stein did.

"Of course, your excellency," came a reply accompanied by a smile because most certainly he knew who Le Loi was. "Le Loi was a great Vietnamese king who established the Le dynasty."

"And...?" Stein urged for more.

The boy's confidence faded. He was at a loss on how to answer. He thought he gave the correct response: The Le dynasty. What more was there to say? Establishing a dynasty was of the highest achievements in Vietnam. What other answer did the governor expect? The boy dared to look at his headmaster with squinting eyes begging for help.

Help came, not from the headmaster, but from Quinn. The gentle and shy student slowly raised his hand, looked directly at Stein, and spoke. With a slow measured pace that developed into a speech infused with self-confidence, Quinn interjected, "Your excellency. Le Loi was indeed a great king, but his greatness was born out of legend." The headmaster clenched his teeth and moved directly behind Quinn, placing his hands on the boy's shoulders, squeezing them, as if to stifle any further response.

Stein waved him away, fascinated by this boy who had the gumption to reply out of turn.

"Please, go on." This gave Quinn added courage even though he was uncertain if his outburst would cost him his future. As he replied, the headmaster released his grip.

"Your excellency, Le Loi began as a simple fisherman." Stein nodded, confirming Quinn's reply and giving him tacit permission to continue.

As Quinn began to relate the legend of Le Loi, all fear left him, and in his subconscious he was transported to a world where Vietnamese legends cast their spell on all those who were enchanted by them.

"One day, as he cast his net upon the lake where he was fishing, his net caught on a very heavy object that lay just beneath the surface." Quinn became animated and he began to gesticulate in order to assist him in telling the tale. "Le Loi pulled on his net very hard, but the object remained fast under water. Holding on to the net, Le Loi paddled his little boat to the site where the object had caught his net. As he bent down to free his net, he saw beneath the water a glimmering object; it was so bright that the surrounding water was lit by its radiance. Le Loi reached for it. It felt very cool to the touch. He pulled. Nothing moved. He pulled harder but the object remained fast. Then, with one great effort, he pulled again, and the object released! Freed from the lake, Le Loi held the object up to the sky. Your excellency, it was a sword!"

"A sword, you say?" Stein queried in mock wonder. Of course, he knew the legend, but he was completely enthralled by Quinn's eloquent and expressive narration of the story.

"Yes, your excellency, a sword. But this was not just any sword. This was an enchanted sword with which he could slay his enemies." At this point, Quinn regained his composure, placed his arms by his side, and with some dread, looked back at his headmaster. He was pleased to see the headmaster's hint of a smile and the slight nod of his head. The headmaster was in fact proud of his shy young protégé, who surprisingly dared to reveal the essence of what it meant to be a Vietnamese.

"Enemies? Tell me boy, who were the enemies of Le Loi?" Stein persisted as he thoroughly enjoyed this young man.

"Why, the Chinese, your excellency. They have always been our enemies."

"And, was Le Loi victorious over his enemies?"

"Oh, yes indeed, your excellency. The humble fisherman became a great warrior. He defeated his enemies and sent them back to the north. Then, he was made emperor and became the founder of the great Le dynasty."

The first boy, who should have given the complete answer, spitefully shifted his eyes toward Quinn; he was angry that this nobody had undermined him. Quinn, infused with a measure of victory, almost as if he were Le Loi himself, then surprised both Stein and the headmaster by elaborating further.

"Your excellency. I believe that the English people have a man similar to Le Loi."

"Really, now." It was more of a statement than a question by the Governor who was completely taken by the young lad.

"Yes, your excellency. I believe the English people call their Le Loi, King Arthur." This reply assured Quinn's fate.

"What is your name, son?" Stein motioned to the secretary to make note of it.

"Quinn Ai Ngoc, your excellency. But, to most, I am known as Quinn."

The Governor nodded his satisfaction. He would hardly recall examining the other boys. Quinn had captivated him. He would be chosen by Stein to continue his education under the tutelage and expense of the government, in France; there was no question about it.

Seldom, if ever, had Stein seen the ability and animation in one so young, regardless of whether he was European or Vietnamese. He was sure that this student, known as Quinn, would succeed. Stein would send this boy to the French school in Tourane where, after he had learned to speak French, he would undergo a vocational aptitude selection, and be placed into a professional school in France. For Quinn, it meant attending medical school; Quinn would become a doctor.

The other boys who had not been chosen would channel their disappointment and rejection into the hands of those who fervently worked to undermine the French. They would migrate to the North and join the forces that would reap havoc on the Colonialists. They would consider Quinn to be a puppet and an instrument of the French; unless, he was reeducated and converted, he would be a targeted for revenge.

5

Politics

René combed through news sources daily for any information regarding the survivors of the fallen colony, particularly the battle of Dien Bien Phu. Very little had been mentioned in the Paris press about the battle itself other than details about the Geneva Accords. Unlike the reports from World War II, the loss of Indochina produced no lists of the dead or wounded.

The agreement in Geneva settled the Indochina matter for France. The colony was lost, as were the men who had fought for it; they had just vanished. The only information available came from the French Communist Party journals circulated in opposition to the government.

Prisoners had been taken, though the journals had been vague about the number, or their location. On a daily basis, René would sit at the Café Faubourg, a place known for its communist sympathies as well as an establishment where Ho Chi Minh himself had once frequented and written his polemics. There, René waited for the latest journal to be circulated. Occasionally, she would also meet Dr. Lebrun as he had become a crucial ally in maintaining her emotional stability; Lebrun was also very absorbed in finding out the latest news about the prisoners and, in particular, about Sal.

Unfortunately for Lebrun, his hospital schedule was much reduced because of his failing eyesight, and he had been forced to take an administrative position. Acting as an administrator neither satisfied him nor provided an outlet for the active life of a surgeon to which he was accustomed. He sorely missed teaching surgery, but as a physician he knew full well that his deteriorating eyesight would put him and his patients at risk in the operating room. His meetings with René provided Lebrun with some solace; together they sought comfort in each other. With time on his hands, he looked forward to meeting with this unpretentiously bright, although melancholy woman. For her part, René found Lebrun's wise guidance a ray of hope in an otherwise bleak existence.

Dr. Lebrun was very well aware of the fickle nature of French politics, particularly when it came to salvaging the remnants of its failed foreign policy. Born into a class of society destined to a measure of success, some of Lebrun's classmates and colleagues had risen to prominence in their professional and political lives; Lebrun had friends in high places. As such, his contacts in the French government kept him abreast of current events.

Lebrun held little hope for learning the fate of the survivors of Dien Bien Phu, especially those men in the country's Foreign Legion. But, for the sake of René, Lebrun kept up a façade of optimism. He saw how her mood would swing the moment a new journal had been published. He noticed how her fingers trembled with the turn of every page. Once she had thoroughly read each article, she would slowly fold up the journal and let it slip into her lap. With each publication, what began as an eager exploration for hope ended in frustration and despondency.

Holding back her tears, René summed up the latest issue of the journal, reporting to Lebrun in an increasingly loud tone, "Once again, nothing. Not a *word*. Nothing but the same ravings over the régime and, of course, the Americans!"

"I'm not able to read as well as I used to, but I'm not deaf, yet." Lebrun replied, trying to inject some humor into the conversation.

"Oh, I'm sorry, I didn't know that I was raising my voice."

Humoring René was futile.

"The Americans? Why are they angry with the Americans?"

"Everyone is cross with the Americans." On this subject, René had become an expert through her daily examination of the news from every source.

"The Communists feel betrayed because the Americans and the Chinese persuaded the Geneva Conference to partition Indochina. Now, the country has been named North Vietnam and South Vietnam."

"But, my dear what upsets our government so about the Americans?" Lebrun had not been privy to this latest squabble between France and America. His sources in the government kept this information to themselves.

René became extremely defensive because Sal was an American.

"The government feels that as an ally, America should have provided military aid as Indochina was going into the toilet. The whole thing is ludicrous, Dr. Lebrun. I was there. I knew how hopeless the situation in that valley was. The Americans could have helped; they should have helped."

Lebrun was quite familiar with the American attitude towards Indochina. He knew that by the time the Colony had collapsed, the Americans were funding most of the war. They had warned the French to give up their Colonial ambitions after the last world war. They predicted what would happen in Indochina.

Dr. Lebrun also frequently thought of Sal. What he knew of Sal was the result of having been his professor; everything else about him came from René. Also, what Lebrun knew about the last battle came from René; he was the only one with whom she would entrust the details of her ordeal in the valley. Lebrun was astonished at her first-hand report as well as at her courage under fire. He knew her to be cool and calm in a controlled medical situation, but when she described the chaos of the battalion aid station, this was beyond anything he had experienced. Of course, the focus of her recollection was Sal, and it was through her eyes that Lebrun began to realize what a remarkable man Sal had become.

Lebrun, distraught at what was becoming of his precious nurse, decided to act. He would use his government contacts to gain as much information as he could and perhaps, encourage them to do something, anything, to discover the fate of the Legionnaires. The question was whether or not to take René into his confidence. Her work at the Descartes was superb, and above all, he wanted to ensure that her nursing skills would not be compromised by the distraction of a plan he was considering. Yet, he could no longer bear to see René suffer; the thought of her desolation had won. He decided to let her in on his plan.

"René, I have some dear friends in the French government. Some people very high up who owe me for some favors I did for them in the past."

Immediately, René became animated. In all their meetings together, Lebrun had never come forward with anything other than a consoling gesture. Now, she sensed that Dr. Lebrun could take some sort of action to find out what had happened to Sal.

"Is there something you can do? Really? I mean, what is it that you can...?" Her questions came one after another, and the flood of her words almost overwhelmed the old man.

"Wait, my dear. Have patience. I have a little plan, but I must be very careful before I can report any progress to you."

"Patience?" René did not mean to be impertinent but, indeed, she had almost run out of patience.

"Yes, my dear. Just a little more tolerance on your part. I know what you are going through and I will try to do what I can. This, I beg of you. I am not as young as I once was, but I have to be very certain of what I am about to do."

"Dr. Lebrun," René spoke as she stood up, realizing that further questioning would be pointless. "I won't ask any more questions. I have always trusted your judgment and will continue to do so. You have given me some hope."

Very formally, René extended her hand as if to shake Dr. Lebrun's before she left. Lebrun gave a little chuckle as instead of shaking her hand, he took it, and as the gentleman he was bred to be, gently touched his lips on the top of one of her fingers and smiled at her.

"René, the only thing worse than the wrath of a woman scorned is the concern of a woman in love." He left the table, stopped, and turned to leave her with a parting hint of comfort.

"I will tell you something the moment I hear anything. I promise you that."

After parting, René, infused with renewed optimism, rushed back to her little apartment pursuing busy work to avoid the crushing thoughts of Sal in peril. For the first time, she was hopeful that she might hear something that could alleviate the relentless feeling of helplessness. What if Lebrun could manage to get information about Sal? What if he and the other captives were alive? But, what if …? These questions consumed her and put her into a manic state as she went about dusting or adjusting furniture repetitively. Finally, exhausted, she sat down and tried to temper her hopefulness; difficult as it was, René finally fell asleep.

Lebrun went straight away to his office and unlocked the bottom drawer of his desk where he kept "private" files. He searched for one particular folder. After fumbling through stacks of paper, he found what he was searching for. It was a medical file on none other than Monsieur Pierre Minot. Lebrun smiled as he scanned the pages, realizing that what he held in his hands represented some leverage. The file he was holding belonged to the Prime Minister of France, a university classmate of Lebrun's. They had maintained their friendship as each had risen to prominence in their respective professions.

Lebrun was determined to make an appointment with his old friend. He knew that the medical file he held in his hands would assure him of being received by the highest authority in the French government. Blackmail between friends was not unusual; it assured advancement as well as maintenance of status in the realm of gentlemen.

The French Parliament building, home to the National Assembly was modeled in the classical Greek style. However, the inner workings of the legislators who occupied posts within were anything but democratic. Fickle, vain, and mostly looking after their own interests, the legislators had long ago abandoned the ideals of liberty, fraternity, and equality. 'Equality' was the first to die, as wealthy deputies heavily invested in Southeast Asia and Africa became the new aristocracy. Those within this latest nobility became innovative predators with unrestricted freedom to rape French colonies. 'Fraternity' became synonymous with the band of thieves who promulgated laws to serve their own purpose. 'Liberty' meant autonomy and safety from prosecution.

The French government, last in the race to colonize, acted with greed and incompetence. France lost more than a colony when Southeast Asia fell; its dignity was misplaced in the eyes of a world that had long given up colonization as a method of acquiring revenue. As a result, the Western global community paid little heed to France during negotiations involving matters of international configuration. The Geneva Accords that ended the Indochina War compelled France to sit in the corner, keep silent, and let the powers that had once been close allies negotiate on its own behalf. After the fall of Dien Bien Phu, French Indochina was neither French nor was there a reference to China in its new name: Vietnam. The peasants who previously bled at the hands of the French, had now done the bloodletting and celebrated victory over the French and, most importantly, colonialism.

Dr. Lebrun was on his way to see the architect of a failed foreign policy that not only abandoned the administrators of Indochina but also the men who had been sent there to defend it. Pierre Minot was not blind, but he had no vison. He should have predicted the outcome of the Indochina War because his National Assembly had long ago lost interest in funding the venture.

Lebrun entered the austere building taking note of the exclusive finishes adorning the interior; Teak, an exotic wood procured from Southeast Asia, lined its halls, each wall skirted with marble, and the finest carpets from Africa giving cushion to the ornate desks that rested on them. In each corridor were shelves holding a vast array of pottery. It resembled an exquisite museum that lacked a capable curator.

Lebrun had phoned ahead to ensure that the Prime Minister was in attendance. A gentle reminder regarding the dossier in his possession assured that the Minister would make time to see him. The echoes of his footsteps followed Lebrun as he presented himself to the reception desk in front of the Prime Minister's chambers.

"Dr. Lebrun." The secretary who knew Lebrun to be an intimate friend of her boss greeted him. "You are expected. Good to see you, again. Please, go right in."

With a faint smile, indicating that he had direct entry, Lebrun opened the massive door leading to the inner sanctum of the French government.

Immediately, Minot stood and rushed to greet his old friend. He led him to the chair normally reserved for diplomats, and they sat facing each other. Brandy was poured and the old doctor accepted it, holding the glass in one hand while stroking the file resting on his lap with the other.

"It's been a long time, my old friend. How are you getting along?" With this question Pierre Minot was really asking the purpose of Lebrun's visit. Minot puffed his cheeks and knew that he was in for a request. He finished his brandy with one mouthful and poured another.

Lebrun paced his plan as was his custom. "Oh, things with me are as usual. Young doctors are becoming harder to train; they think they know everything. They are very difficult to reign in." A chain of perceptible beads of sweat appeared on Minot's brow; with the file on Lebrun's lap, Minot wanted him to get to the point without the pleasantries of chitchat.

"Yes, I suppose medicine is changing all the time; all the new machines and such." Minot's foot was tapping slightly as his eyes never wavered from the file. Lebrun felt that the response was polite; still, he wanted Minot to squirm a little until the time was ripe.

The two men sat like this for twenty minutes, recalling the "good old" university days, that after consideration by both, were not so good after all; Minot sparring, Lebrun hedging. Finally, Minot broke the invisible wall and brought Dr. Lebrun to the subject of his visit.

"So, my dear friend, what can I do for you?" He asked, giving a nod to Lebrun's file.

Lebrun, considering that the time had come to be direct, set his glass down and kept the promise he had made to René.

"Pierre," Lebrun began by addressing his friend by name and not title, "I am here to inquire about the French prisoners captured at Dien Bien Phu."

"Who?" Squinting his eyes, Minot replied as if he had never heard of the battle. Indeed, he had heard of the end of Indochina. After all, he had signed the document in Geneva that ended the war.

Lebrun stroked the file as if to refresh the Prime Minister's memory.

"Surely you recall Dien Bien Phu?" Lebrun realized that the Minister's avoidance to the question represented the same evasion practiced by the country as it ignored defeat and to its shame, surrendered men without preparing to receive them back and bind their wounds.

"Pierre, the men that were left behind after Dien Bien Phu. What became of them?"

"Oh, those fellows."

"Yes, those fellows." Lebrun confirmed that no effort had been expended to repatriate the men who had defended and sacrificed their lives for the lost colony.

Minot had signed the accords that brought the war to an end. He had signed the provision that would bring humane treatment to the men who had been captured. The war ended in May; it was now August. Lebrun was furious at the "those fellows" statement, but his strategy would not come to fruition if he lost control.

"Yes, those fellows", Lebrun repeated in a somber tone. "I am here to inquire about those fellows." There was no way of evading the question; Minot's eyes never left the folder on Lebrun's lap.

"Well, my dear friend, as you know this Dien Bien Phu region is most difficult to communicate with. Even the commanding general has no idea of what really happened there. Of course, it is my understanding that most of the men there were Legionnaires."

"Legionnaires who fought for France." Lebrun shot back. The use of the past tense made it obvious to Lebrun that Minot and his government had abandoned them. Slowly, Lebrun took up the file from his lap and opened it, fingering the pages. Then, for emphasis, he flicked a finger on a selected page. The Prime Minister began to sweat; he poured himself another brandy.

The file that Lebrun had, was indeed, leverage to be used against his old friend. It signified a treatment plan that many Frenchmen had undergone both in their youth as well as in their present circumstances. Illicit sexual liaisons were part of French politics; sexual perversion, however, was not. Minot's file, held by his old friend and doctor, was confidential at the moment. Minot knew it. So many indiscretions should be kept private but end up in the tabloids; Minot knew that as well. He was, however, confident that his old friend Lebrun would keep the file in his desk under lock and key; it was but a matter of fulfilling a request by Lebrun that would maintain his secret.

"Well, my friend, I believe the French Army is in control of repatriating their own. The matter is solely in their hands." Minot tried an excuse that he knew would not satisfy Lebrun.

"Surely, as Prime Minister, you must have some knowledge of the progress being made. It's been three months since the end of the war." This was more of a rebuke than a question. Lebrun was determined to remind his old friend of his sworn duties as the head of state.

"I have left the matter solely to the army. I do know the army men have been repatriated."

"Yes, of course, the army men. What of the Legionnaires? Are they not part of the French Army?"

"Well, yes," Minot hesitated. "But, these men are not entirely French."

Lebrun could no longer contain his anger. The file in his hands began to quiver.

"Minot, I am very interested in the whereabouts of the men who were captured at Dien Bien Phu. My understanding from excellent sources is that the Legionnaires were captured. These were brave and honorable men. If the French Army did not recognize their bravery, you and your government should. You have the opportunity to preserve some measure of honor for the country."

Minot knew what Lebrun wanted. He must have some connection to the men who had been captured. Still, he tried to compensate for his government's oversight.

"This Indochina thing was a nasty business. We should have left a long time ago." He poured himself another drink, anticipating what would come next.

"They might be Legionnaires and Colonials, but nonetheless, they are still our men and you have a responsibility for them."

"What exactly can I do for you, my friend? Give me the specifics please." The time for evasion was over.

"I would like for you to see the President and start the wheels in motion in order to bring these men home." To Minot's surprise, Lebrun offered the file to him. "I want to see those men come home and out of harm's way." Minot reached for the file. At last, this evidence would disappear if he could help Lebrun. This was more of an order than a request. As if to drive his point home, Lebrun continued.

"You can drink your brandy in the evenings while those men languish in some godforsaken jungle. Your subordinates can go about their daily bureaucratic nonsense, while those men suffer, wither and die. You can forget these men, but I will not." With that, Lebrun handed the file over to Minot.

Puzzled, yet relieved, Minot questioned his old friend.

"Why is this so important to you? Surely, you are not talking about honor?"

"My concern is not about honor. You and this government put that in the toilet a long time ago. I made a promise to a dear friend, and I mean to keep it. Will you help me keep it, or not?"

Minot went to his desk and locked up the file as he reached for the phone.

"Marie? Yes. Please call the President and ask him to arrange a meeting with me. Yes. Yes, it is quite urgent. Thank you." Wiping the sweat from his forehead, Minot looked earnestly at Lebrun. "Are you satisfied?"

Lebrun was pleased. Perhaps something could now be done for those forgotten few. Hopefully, Sal would still be among them. He offered his hand to the Prime Minister. "One good turn deserves another. Bring those men back and I'll give you the rest of the pages in that file." Relief drained from Minot's face as Lebrun turned and walked out of the office.

As he left the Parliament and walked among an oblivious Parisian population pursuing their daily routine, Lebrun thought to himself. "Nasty business, that's what he called it." From what René had told him about Indochina over the past weeks, Minot had no inkling of what 'nasty' meant. Lebrun's brief visit to the halls of government convinced him that France alone went against the flow of history. France isolated itself from the reality of the modern world, and Indochina held on to an idea whose time had become extinct. "Nine years", Lebrun pondered. "Such futility and waste of lives! Sal might be among them. Not knowing why, Minot was right. It was a nasty business." By the time Lebrun reached the hospital, it was evening. He knew that René was consumed with grief. She would be creating a fantasy in which Sal, alive, would come back to her. Perhaps the visit to his old friend would bear fruit, and René's dream might become reality; perhaps.

6

Restoration

Sal, semi-delirious, woke up no longer cradled in the arms of the Sergeant Major. Instead, he was in the care of Quinn in his private quarters. To evade suspicion from the Political Officers, who seemed to be everywhere in the camp, Quinn told them that he had to care personally for the Legionnaire "doctor" in order to keep him alive; he was essential in helping care for the wounded.

Quinn was encouraged as new orders had arrived from Hanoi. Negotiated at the highest levels of the defeated French government, the wounded were to be cared for in a humane manner and repatriated to France. The Vietminh had refused to sign the Geneva Accords because their country had been denied independence and divided in half. Even more provoking, the international community recognized Vietnam as consisting of a North and a South; a nation divided by ideology. North Vietnam was to be controlled by the Communists, and South Vietnam was to be supervised by a democratic republic and allied with the Americans.

The torment of war may have ended, but now the overwhelming result was paranoia. The North Vietnamese felt that since they had won the war against the French, then they should have been the ones to dictate the conditions for capitulation at Geneva. Instead, in order to weaken Vietnam, their old enemy China, in concert with the United States, who had assumed financial responsibility for the war, manipulated the Geneva agreement to include partition of the country. To the people of the North and Ho Chi Minh, the settlement represented the ultimate diplomatic double cross. Vietnam's dream of independence had been shattered on a conference table in Switzerland.

However, in order to keep diplomatic channels open, the president of North Vietnam, Ho Chi Minh, thought it best to comply with one of the articles in the Geneva agreement: the humane treatment of prisoners of war. Hanoi conveyed this order to the camp, and the Political Officers had no choice but to submit. As a result, Quinn's ruse to care for Sal privately made sense to the Political cadre who suspected sedition from everyone and everything; therefore, reluctantly, they left their doctor alone to do his best.

Sal, severely undernourished, weighed one hundred and twenty pounds when Quinn assumed care for him. The young man had lost most of his weight as a result of starvation, diarrhea, and vomiting. The pressing problem for Quinn was not only to treat Sal's wretched state of malnourishment, complicated by malaria, but also to treat the beriberi that was slowly rotting his body away. The first signs of the disease appeared on the trail; Sal's gums began to bleed until his teeth became so loose that, had he the strength to cough, he would have spit out several of them. Then, the skin on his arms and legs developed ulcerations, craters filled with pus, attracting a host of flies.

Quinn procured some limes and pineapples that were abundant in the camp. He ground them up, added water, and made a broth. Within days, Sal's gums became hard and his teeth were no longer loose. Healing from multiple insults to the body under normal conditions is a complicated task. In the tropics, without the benefit of proper medicine, recovery of the seriously ill is significantly impaired. Quinn, however, was not only schooled in western medicine, he also had a good knowledge of medicine as practiced by the Chinese. Antibiotics, predominantly sulfa, were available in the camp, but restricted for use on Vietnamese patients. Quinn very carefully secreted small quantities of sulfa as he made his rounds through the Viet huts. The Political Officers were watchful and suspicious, but Quinn was able to measure out an amount of the powder that would help Sal recover more quickly. Of chief concern were the ulcerations on Sal's skin that festered unabated in the tropical heat; sulfa powder would heal these but would do nothing for the fever and delirium caused by the malaria.

Malaria, the silent parasite, would awaken in cycles, causing convulsions; as quickly as it caused physical pandemonium, the parasite would abate, and the patient would find some relief. For this ailment, Quinn extracted quinine from the bark of trees. He ground up the bark and mixed it with coconut milk. Teaspoon after teaspoon, he fed Sal like a baby until the fever became manageable. All the while, the Political Officers demanded to know when the French "doctor" would be able to assist. Quinn, using medical jargon not understood by the officers, reassured them that it would be just a matter of time.

After a week of Quinn's treatment, Sal slowly responded and regained his senses. First, his eyes were able to focus; the fog that clouded his vision disappeared. Then, his hearing improved along with his sense of taste. Perhaps, the prime benefit of Quinn's healing came when Sal, in between the fevers that no longer raged, was able to recognize the man who not only treated him but had also protected him.

"Quinn!" Sal managed a smile through parched lips that bled when stretched. "Quinn, my God, it's you!"

Quinn smiled, revealing a mouth full of gold teeth. He let loose with a flood of tears as his old roommate recognized him.

"Yes, my old friend. It is Quinn, your schoolmate."

Sal managed one more moment of lucidity before he drifted off into a healing slumber and mumbled, "And, my old friend."

Sal's dreams became more defined, no longer a miasma of jumbled visions. And dreaming such, his health slowly became restored as shards of memory slowly began to coalesce; his reminiscences became distinct recollections. As his health returned, so did his optimism, which hastened the return of his strength. Step by step, day by day, Sal recalled the journey that brought him to the hut in the North Vietnamese jungle and finally into the arms of his friend.

Sal recalled his early days in New York City, where his voyage began. Flashes of his mother and her slow descent into madness overcame him. She had replaced him with a cat. He realized that nothing he ever did or would ever do could please her. Sal couldn't conjure an image of his father: a father who had been a shadow, was now an unrecognizable ghost in his memory.

Behind the declining fevers, Sal also remembered what had spirited him away from the city he detested. It had started with his inattentiveness and poor attendance in school, which led to his eventual expulsion. Then, there was Bud, the wrinkled old seaman who lived behind the Camel sign in Times Square. Bud was Sal's inspiration to become a merchant seaman and gave Sal the opportunity to embark upon his great adventure at sea.

During Sal's more lucid moments, while being fanned and fed quinine by Quinn, he thought about the S.S. Washington, the ship that had taken him away from New York and the misery of his young life. Fond memories of Chee, the Chinese cook who had protected him from an aggressive and ruthless crew, made him smile as he recalled the Chinaman's broken English. Of course, how could he forget the captain of his ship, the aristocrat who had taken an interest in him and in his education by offering to him the books Sal had once rejected.

Sleep carried Sal away from recalling the accidental death of a fellow seaman who had wanted to harm him, the subsequent running through the streets of Marseilles, and his serendipitous meeting of Avram in the Legion recruiting station. The memory of Avram stirred him awake and brought a smile to his haggard face. Avram, his best friend, was the Holocaust survivor who taught Sal how to survive as well.

Now, healthy and awake, Sal reminisced over the circumstances that led the two of them to join the French Foreign Legion and eventually becoming close, like brothers. Certainly, also, there was Jaehne, the grizzled veteran German sergeant who reluctantly took the two of them under his wing; trial by fire, made him a brother, as well. Finally, the most horrific memory of all brought Sal to the full realization of where he was now, and how he had arrived there. The jump into darkness, the fall of Dien Bien Phu, and the sight of his brothers, Jaehne and Avram, as they lay in the mud: one, mutilated beyond recognition, and the other, who had been shot in the back as he ran from the defeated column.

What completed Sal's recovery, however, was not just the quinine and sulfa. The remedy that motivated Sal to live was his memory of René. He recalled her gentle voice as she advocated for him and encouraged him when he was a student shunned by his classmates. He could almost sense the softness and warmth of her touch as the two of them became acquainted at their café. He recalled the sweet scent of her perfume when he kissed her hand; he could smell it even now in the stifling heat of the hut. When at last he was able to stand, his strength came from the conviction of René's love for him. It was the memory of René that brought him out from the darkness of delirium and into the light hope for a future with René. The thought of her infused him with a desire to survive; to see her, and hold her, once again.

Alert, Sal fully appreciated his dire situation. He noted the mildew inside the hut and felt the pervasiveness of the powdery red dust that coated his body. When he could eat solid food, he tasted the overpowering Nuoc Mam fish sauce that the Vietnamese used liberally on everything they ate. Throughout Sal's entire ordeal, Quinn remained by his side, measuring his progress daily. Quinn stroked Sal's forehead and wiped away the sickly sweat produced by the malaria. Quinn fed him, partly from his own rations. There were no words that could express Sal's gratitude.

"Quinn, I thought I was dead."

"You almost were, my friend, but you are strong, and fate has an agenda. You played your part well." A broad golden smile reassured Sal that he was in safe hands. "I am not your enemy, in spite of the uniform that I wear. Your real enemy surrounds you and we must be careful. If I command you, if I raise my voice at you, it is merely an act in order to keep you safe. We have won this war Sal, but my people now embark upon a war of reunification. We will keep on fighting until we are finally independent."

Sal did not understand. He had been insensible during the events that occurred in Geneva. He was unaware of the subsequent betrayal and dissatisfaction of the Vietnamese.

"But I thought you were content with your little hospital in Quang Tri." Sal recalled the last time that he and René had seen Quinn.

Quinn changed the subject quickly. "My friend, this is no time to talk of politics. It is not safe, and in the long run, I don't think you would understand the situation that we or my people are in."

Sal did not respond. He was puzzled. He remembered Quinn working in the Quang Tri hospital. He thought that he was happy there: at peace. What Sal had not been aware of, however, was that many of the patients in that hospital, the ones whose sheets were drawn up to their necks to hide their uniforms, were enemy soldiers with wounds inflicted by the French. Sal was also unaware that Quinn's country of Vietnam had been suffering from wounds imposed on it by a long list of foreigners including the Chinese, Japanese and of course, the French. Sal knew none of this; how could he? He was not even aware that Quinn, his medical school roommate in Paris and the doctor who had been trained by the French, had all the while sympathized with his own countrymen.

"I will explain everything to you after you have recovered fully and when it is safe to do so." Quinn's soft tone calmed Sal. He chose to savor the joy of reuniting with his friend and leave further questions for a later time. Sal knew that Quinn would clarify everything in time.

When Sal stepped outside of Quinn's hut to take a look at his surroundings, a Political Officer immediately approached, gesticulating and screaming at him. Quinn intervened, nodded his head several times and, turning to Sal, began to translate.

"He says that it is time for you to work." In a lower voice he added, "Watch out for this one. We must do as he says."

Quinn briefed Sal on what to expect in the camp and what his medical duties would be. At first, the two would work together, and Quinn would teach Sal how to extract quinine as well as other non-traditional medical techniques that were necessary due to the lack of medicine. After a week, Sal would be on his own. As a precaution, Quinn would arrange for Sal to treat the Vietnamese; this might instill some measure of trust in him by the Political Officers.

The enormity and scope of misery that Sal encountered as he began to make rounds with Quinn were staggering. It was as if his walking on the trail was a dream, he had slept in delirium, and had suddenly awakened to see the vast number of huts containing the ill and dying.

In time, the Vietnamese increased the availability of medicine as they were under pressure from their headquarters to keep as many of the prisoners alive as possible. Harassment by the guards decreased, and the availability of food increased. The prisoners soon appreciated any meal that would sustain them.

Quinine in any form was a great benefit in treating malaria; with Quinn's guidance, Sal learned how to extract and administer the healing substance to everyone who needed it. Soon, fevers abated, and the prisoners began to thrive. Some were able to ambulate. There was no thought of escape. There was simply nowhere to escape unnoticed: a white face among the Vietnamese would soon be detected.

The prisoners, like phantoms, emerged from their huts to search for friends that might have survived. Sal was naturally a welcome sight to them, not only because of the service he provided but also because he was one of them. Quinn was tolerated because of his position, but it was Sal, who was recognized by the Legionnaires as their doctor.

On a daily basis, Quinn and Sal would make their rounds, first, among the Vietnamese then on to the Legionnaires. The death toll began to decline, as did the symptoms of other diseases that could shorten lives. Native fruits from the jungle became a staple at every meal; relieving the ravages of beriberi as well as a host of other tropical diseases that were due to vitamin deficiency.

Within weeks, senior officers who were still alive began to instill some measure of discipline in those that were able to gather into a military formation; roll call gave the officers an approximation of who had been spared and who had been committed to the flames of the pit. The

Vietnamese patients also began to recover, and along with the Political Officers, participated in the daily formal military ritual of accepting a report from their captives, who were emerging from a nightmare.

When the healthy soldiers outnumbered the ill, the senior Legionnaire officers realized that they were being kept alive for a reason. Some negotiation to which they were not a party must have occurred; this gave them the confidence to inquire as to the conditions of their captivity. Quinn, one of the few Vietnamese that could understand and speak French, performed the duties of a translator during the exchanges between the camp commander and the senior Legion officer. His fluency in the language of the defeated, however, increased suspicion of him among the political cadre.

One month after their arrival, a critical exchange between the victors and their captives occurred. In ragged, disheveled, and shredded uniforms, the Legionnaire contingent marched to the parade ground, looking as martial as they could under their circumstances. There, they faced a contingent of Vietnamese soldiers, along with Political Officers and Quinn, and proceeded to execute a delicate parade ground diplomacy.

Salutes were exchanged. The senior Legion officer, still reeling from the effects of malaria and standing on unsteady legs, inquired:

"Sir. We are grateful for the kindness you have shown us and, in particular, the treatment that has been rendered by your doctor." After translation by Quinn, one Political Officer glared at him; Quinn had been placed in an untenable position.

"I would like to inquire as to the status of my men and any information that you can communicate to us regarding our future," the senior Legion officer continued.

The camp commandant replied, speaking directly to Quinn, "Tell him that we have been informed by Hanoi that they are in direct discussions with his government. Also, tell him that I believe that they will all be repatriated, soon." Quinn translated.

A hint of a smile on the face of the Legion officer led to a brisk salute. As he did an about-face, still on shaky legs, Sal came up to steady him. The Vietnamese contingent left, along with Quinn who thought it prudent not to remain, thereby incurring further suspicion regarding his loyalty.

For the first time since before the first shell landed on Dien Bien Phu, joy erupted among the exhausted men who had fought there bravely. As they received the news from their commander, feeble attempts to throw their hats in the air were accompanied by gentle caresses of men who could barely stand in formation. As the men dispersed, all were infused with the hope that they would soon be returned to France. Sal remained alone on the parade ground looking towards Quinn who briefly, turned to meet Sal's gaze. They each wondered if they would ever see one another again

7

Welcome Home

By maritime safety standards, the S.S. Washington was unfit to sail. The old merchant vessel had been in service since World War I and had never been refitted or updated except for a coating of paint; even the paint had worn thin as rust multiplied like a fungus. At one time, its captain had been an outcast from a family that could have owned several fleets. His life at sea, however, gave him the satisfaction of not having to compete with avaricious siblings, or meeting the expectations of a patriarch who had no use for a son who lived the life of a conventional sea captain. Upon the captain's death, the ship seemed to have died as well; successors to the helm were transient seamen with little discipline or interest in maintaining the vessel.

The chief boatswain's mate, a dwarf whose ability to run the ship far exceeded his size, had retired. Mr. Fitzgerald had decided that after years at sea, the constant separation from land had worn him out. So, he decided to look up an old mate, Bud, who had previously served with him, and retired in New York City. Bud had been a maintenance worker who lived behind the Camel sign in Times Square, keeping the smoke ring cannon in repair as it blew smoke rings out and over the city's landmark intersection.

It was Bud who had motivated Sal to go to sea. For a while, Bud had moved away to find work elsewhere, but like the sea, the Camel sign had a mystical attraction for him and drew him back to his quarters behind the landmark. In a sense, he was the watchman of Times Square. As Bud and Fitzgerald had each known Sal, who had once sailed as a merchant seaman with Fitzgerald on the S.S. Washington, the subject of his whereabouts became a constant topic of discussion. Neither one of them had any idea that, at that very moment, Sal, along with the rest of the survivors of Dien Bien Phu, were on the docks of Haiphong in North Vietnam, waiting for transport back to France.

Ten freighters leased by the French government were docked at Haiphong to return what was left of their Legion soldiers to France; the S.S. Washington was among them. Three thousand men, most of them Legionnaires, were sitting on the decrepit wooden docks waiting to be repatriated. Another seven thousand had died, either on the march, or in the camps. As a final act of humiliation, the Vietnamese had dressed the prisoners in pink cotton pajamas adorned with broad black stripes. Even though the men were about to be freed, there was no joy or celebration. Some were still ill, others damaged beyond repair; all of them were worn out.

Because of Quinn, Sal was healthier than most, and as a result, he was permitted to wander in between rows of the sick who had been quarantined and separated from the rest. Most of his time was taken up with delousing: blessing the men with white powder that would kill anything that crawled on the withered and parched bodies. In truth, killing lice saved energy; time was better spent reaching for water buckets left by the Vietnamese among the dehydrated troops who sat in the intense heat without benefit of shade. The slight breeze from the Gulf of Tonkin made little difference; the men baked. Sal had not been provided with any medicine to administer to the ill. So close to finally being released, it was Sal's reassurance that saw the men through the long-awaited boarding onto the freighters, and hopefully, to a safe haven.

Since an agreement had been reached with the French, it was in the best interest of the Vietnamese to spare as many of the surviving prisoners as they could; in any event, they would soon be rid of the whole lot. No one, not even the Legionnaires knew how many of their comrades had been captured or killed. The Vietnamese kept no records but were aware that as time progressed for their charges in captivity, it became easier to feed those who survived.

At last, Vietnamese soldiers began to blow whistles and prod the sitting prisoners awake and to their feet. It was time to board. Divided into rows, men slowly began to make their way up the ramps and onto the vessels. They were ushered by completely disinterested crewmembers down into the holds of the ship. Descending on shaking ladders whose rust flakes peed off with each hand hold, the men entered what appeared to be an iron prison. The steel walls were covered with sea sweat, smelling of mold and salt. At the bottom, littered with remnants of rice left over from the previous cargo, rudimentary tiered bunks, eight stacked upon each other, had been hastily prepared. There, without benefit of mattresses or padding, the healthiest of men would claim top bunks while those who were ill and suffering from dysentery crawled onto the bottom. The holds were used to carrying cargo, not men. Toilet facilities consisted of a row of buckets hardly sufficient for the three hundred souls that occupied each steel cavity. The heat of the day was magnified by the iron walls surrounding the men who felt they had entered yet another form of captivity. Unsympathetic crews, Europeans all, hardly spoke to their human cargo.

With great irony, Sal boarded the S.S. Washington, the very same ship that initiated his great adventure. This ship, however, was vastly different from the one on which he had left New York; there was no sense of joy or anticipation. There was not one familiar face among the sullen crew. The landmarks of the ship that he remembered so well were unrecognizable; rust and decayed metal claimed everything that had once been maintained in great order. Looking up at the bridge where Sal had spent so many hours as the helmsman, he saw a different captain, who looked at the boarding men with disdain. As Sal climbed down into his assigned hold, he saw the conditions to which he and his comrades would be subjected; Sal wondered how many would survive this voyage. Except for the occasional cough or retching, the hold was quiet. Muffled commands of "Let all lines loose," combined with the increased throbbing sounds of the engines foretold the ship's departure. Sal could feel the ship moving as it slipped its moors, clearing the docks, and making its way into the Gulf of Tonkin and ultimately, into the South China Sea. Sal's great Indochina adventure had come to an end. His dream of becoming a soldier had come to fruition. He felt neither glory, nor honor. Instead, defeated and alone, Sal wondered what lay ahead for him.

The ship's course had been carefully plotted by the French government to avoid major population centers in an attempt to conceal its cargo; demonstrating a total lack of honor and respect for the men who had given their all for France. They returned as if they were pariahs. The course was set to take them south to Malaysia, through the Strait of Malacca, and into the Indian Ocean. There was to be no respite from the heat that intensified as the ships traveled north into the Red Sea and through the Suez Canal. Orders were that the ship should not dock at any port and fueling would occur offshore.

The human cargo did receive some unexpected benefits from the constant ration of oatmeal. The oats stemmed the proliferation of dysentery, and, in most cases, put the bowels of the afflicted to rest. Sal became the intermediary between his company and a hostile crew, who remained unresponsive in facilitating any mercy for his men. Two of the Legionnaires eventually died of heat stroke, and after a hasty, unceremonious burial at sea, at Sal's urging, men were allowed on deck and beneath a tarp in order to breathe the fresh air. As water became more plentiful, the men slowly recovered their strength. Sal's shepherding of the ill did not go unnoticed. Officers, most of whom were weak and unable to command, took note of their only medical provider, and would in the future remember his service to them and their men.

As soon as the ship entered the Mediterranean, men were ordered to resume their places in the hold. The captain feared that this familiar body of water would encourage men to jump ship, particularly those who had come from Libya, Tunisia and Morocco; these countries had been fertile recruitment centers for the Legion.

Finally, after a month at sea, withstanding the rigors of heat, the monotonous diet, and the continuous shuddering and vibration of the ship, the S.S. Washington, along with nine other ships, docked at their final destination: Marseilles. The ships moored at the "new docks", away from the city's picturesque harbor. A command sputtered over the loudspeaker of each ship instructing the weary men to disembark. Two thousand eight hundred and seventy-two silent Legionnaires, those who had survived the final leg of their journey home, slowly walked in single file down the ships' gangways without protest. They were directed into one enormous open warehouse that swallowed them whole; these men simply had no will left. The reception these brave Legionnaires received was contrary to what any country would give to those who had upheld the honor of its nation to the best of their ability. There were no bands, no flags, and no loved ones to greet them. The men were ushered into rows by a nondescript French Army officer, not of the Legion, who barked his commands at the Legionnaires through a megaphone that echoed loudly throughout the cavernous building.

"Take off your garments." This short, simple order resulted in each man disrobing and kicking aside his hated prison garb. This symbol of degradation was exchanged for even more humiliation as over two thousand men stood naked, standing at attention, awaiting further orders.

"In front of me are bins containing your new clothes. Each of you, as quickly as possible, take a shirt, pants, socks, and shoes. Sizes are variable and you might not get the fit you need; you can exchange them with your mates at a later time."

The bins contained khaki military articles, but they were not Legion uniforms. This caused general unrest and alarm among men who had been trained to take pride in maintaining their regiment's individuality as exemplified by its uniform. Again, the megaphone shrieked.

"Attention. These clothes are temporary. You will be issued uniforms when you are reunited with your units."

The grumbling ceased as the officer held out the possibility that the men, at some future point, might be transported back to their regiments to be received as soldiers and men of honor. The final blow to morale came from a Legion colonel who briskly marched into the warehouse and assumed his position on one of the upturned clothing bins. He was introduced by the megaphone, and the men were called to attention. For the first time since a semblance of military order had been displayed in the camps, men snapped to attention, faced forward, and fixed their eyes upon the colonel. This was a Legion officer: one of their own. Surely, he would put an end to the disgraceful greeting they had thus far received. There was no prologue of "welcome home." Indeed, what he proceeded to say mortified the men who expected some morsel of military courtesy.

"I have been ordered by the Ministry of Defense to discharge all of you from service." This brought about an immediate response of disbelief.

"I would remind you that you are still at attention," the megaphone squealed as the colonel's voice objected to disorder. "Let me explain further. Those of you who wish to remain in the Legion will be given the opportunity to re-enlist at your present rank. But you are to take a new assumed name. All record of your service in Indochina will be obliterated. French Indochina no longer exists; therefore, your service there must be disregarded."

France had taken the final step to disengage itself from its former colony. Not only had it lost the colony by virtue of mismanagement, but now it intended to separate itself from the men who bled for it. The memory of French Indochina was to be completely expunged from its national conscience even as honor was set aside.

"Those of you who wish to re-enlist, remain in place and the clerks will initiate your paperwork. While your rank will be maintained, any decorations that you have earned in Indochina will be nullified. Those of you who wish to be released from service, please accept our gratitude. We have arranged for you to receive your final stipend according to your rank and time in service. Form a line outside. The clerks will pay you and arrange for transportation to Paris. Once there, you are free to go."

Sal could not believe what he had just heard. He had no particular allegiance to France, but to be deserted by the Legion was unimaginable. How could these regiments in which he had taken so much pride desert him? What happened to the tradition of "looking after our own?" It was historical. The Legion always protected the honor of its men. Now, he was being asked to forget history. In point of fact, he was being asked to forget his best friends, Avram and Jaehne, who had sacrificed their lives, if not for France, then for the Legion. Sal could not comprehend such a thing. His bewilderment was interrupted by a man standing next to him.

"What are you going to do, mate? I guess we have to decide. I got drunk the last time I made this choice; no time for that I suppose."

"We have to decide, now?" Sal asked in a fog of confusion, his mind still muddled by what the colonel had said.

"Yes, mate. Shit or get off the pot. I'm going to re-up. Got no other place to go."

This brought Sal to the reality of having to make a decision, immediately. He quickly tried to weigh his options. His hands became scales on which he placed the pros and cons of leaving or remaining. On the one hand, he placed being deserted by the regiment he loved. On top of that, he included his memories of Avram and Jaehne, and their adventures together. He then thought of what the man next to him had said, "I have no other place to go." But Sal did have a place to go. He had something that most of the others did not have. René. Finally, he pondered over whether or not he was forsaking the path he had chosen for himself. No, he decided; that path had forsaken him. The Legion had subverted itself to a corrupt ideal. Its history would never be the same.

"I'm out." Sal said to the man who was heading for re-enlistment; he merely shrugged his shoulders.

Sal looked around the great hollow. Men were separating into groups. Hands were shaken, backs slapped, and occasionally some men embraced. Sal had no one to say goodbye to; his friends had been left in the valley, dead, renounced by those who had defended it.

Slowly, Sal moved outside and into the line of men who had chosen to be discharged, to accept final payment, and a ticket to Paris. He looked back into the warehouse, gazing at men who appeared to be reanimated because they were about to pick up their lives where they had left them: the valley of Dien Bien Phu.

Dien Bien Phu marked the end of his great adventure in uniform. As he reached the paymaster to sign his discharge papers, Sal fervently hoped that a new one was about to begin, with René.

8

Medical School

The train made several stops along the route from Marseilles to Paris, giving Sal time to reflect. He didn't focus so much on where he had been, but more so upon where he would go from here. René was utmost in his thoughts and that brought forward a host of other concerns. They would be together: that was a certainty. How he would support her and their life together was another matter. His surgical skills were only relevant in the military. He had the ability to practice trauma medicine, but did not have the traditional medical education and professional certifications required of a surgeon. His experience in the military would not substitute for formal medical training in the civilian world. It was one thing to operate under the auspices of the Legion, but now as a civilian, he had to conform and meet the standards required to practice medicine.

He became a citizen of France; as a result of having served the required minimum of five years in the French Foreign Legion. Under American law, anyone who joined a foreign army would lose his U.S. citizenship. So, returning to America was no longer an option for Sal. Besides, there was nothing for him there. His experience in the Legion had Europeanized him and his world view had been vastly expanded. America would remain a part of his past.

There were other passengers on the train who wore the loosely fitted khaki clothing issued by the Legion in Marseilles. They sat alone and seemed lost in their thoughts. They neither acknowledged one another nor attempted to renew the camaraderie that had previously been the hallmark of Legionnaires. Each of them, as Sal was doing, thought about his future outside of the Legion. No longer men of arms, they had to find a way to reintegrate into a society that was alien to them. Many of them could not or would not be assimilated, and would eventually migrate to recruiting centers, returning to the Legion; the only place they could ever feel welcome and-- 'at home'.

The monotonous syncopated rhythm of the train continued as it made its way north, carrying with it a sleepless Sal. By morning, the train entered a Paris that was in full bloom; Spring was a welcome sight to Parisians who filled the terraces of cafés. René sat in her usual place at the Café Faubourg, caring little about the blooming flowers or the lovers strolling on the Rue Mouffetard. Dr. Lebrun had told her about the government's negotiations with the Vietnamese and that repatriation was under way. But she still had no word as to whether Sal was still alive, or not. As much as she wanted to, her anguish and disillusionment prevented her from scouring the newspapers for word of returning Legionnaires. She just stared at her coffee, lost in thoughts of happier days when she and Sal had sat there together.

René sensed him before she saw him. A quiver in the back of her neck revealed that someone was standing near her. Sal had not forgotten her scent; he could not believe that he was standing behind René, breathing the same air as she. Not wanting to cause alarm, he gently placed his hands on her shoulders. She did not startle-- she had not forgotten his touch. René stared straight ahead and slowly put her hands over his. Sal closed his eyes, filled with tears, as he heard the voice that had for so long been confined to his dreams—become real.

"I've been waiting for you," She cried, as tears flooded her eyes and her body delighted in the expectation that she had anticipated for so long. Sal was at a loss for words. He tenderly squeezed her shoulders until she stood, turned, and faced him. What she saw gave her pause: he was haggard and emaciated, which was magnified by the oversized clothing draped over his depleted frame. The initial shock of his appearance quickly dissolved as she raised her hands to caress his exhausted face and drew him towards her. It was her Sal! Their kiss was not a passionate greeting, but one of tenderness; their lips merely brushing against each other, first seeking, then confirming the reality that at last they had found each other.

The scene did not go unnoticed by the patrons sitting nearby. Although they were unaware of the details, they knew that something extraordinary was occurring. The crowd in turn began to clap their hands in admiration of the unlikely pair of lovers. As if the light applause was an approval for them to embrace, they did so; each with their eyes closed, desperately stemming the flow of tears, and struggling to erase the months that had kept them apart.

The little apartment on the Rue Mouffetard remained exactly as Sal had remembered it. While in captivity he had imagined the rooms and the view from the window overlooking the Left Bank of Paris. Now, he was there, sitting on the sofa with René next to him, looking as if she were waking from a nightmare and feeling her way back to reality. She could not refrain from taking his hand and holding it to her lips; touching him as if to confirm this was not a dream.

"You look so thin. My God, what did they do to you?" Sal reached for her fingers, kissing the palm of her hand as she leaned in to him. He too wanted to linger, bathe in her scent, and feel her touch.

"Never mind about all that," said Sal. "In a few weeks, everything will be back the way it was."

But it would not be the same as it had been. He was no longer in the Legion. He had no possibility of earning a living. He had been disconnected from his homeland. Soon, he would explain all of this to her, but for now it was time to live in the present with each other. They would live what they had fantasized and turn it into a reality.

She reached for his hand and slowly led him to the bedroom.

Standing in front of the bed, she touched his shirt, needing only to unfasten the collar button, as it easily fell to the floor. René could now see just how emaciated he was. Tracing her fingers around his ribs she remembered his body the first time she had seen it in Quang Tri: muscular and tanned, with beads of sweat on his chest. She curled her hands around his waist and slowly pulled him to her, undoing the rope that held his trousers. His body hardened and she could see that he was ready for her. In turn, she kneeled on the bed while stroking his hair and touching his forehead with hers, as he, with trembling fingers undid the buttons of her dress that softly slipped away. They slowly reclined onto the bed, touching each other, recalling the first time they had made love in the sunlight filtering through the palm-thatched hut of Quang Tri. But this was not Quang Tri. This was miles and years away from their first experience of tenderness.

Their kisses, gentle and warm at first, became more fervent. The passion that had been kept at bay awakened and erupted into an ethereal series of embraces, intertwined with attempts to melt into each other. Neither had ever experienced the intensity of this erotic beauty. Each caress caused a tremor to bodies that had been denied tenderness and longed to be consumed. Neither had ever heard the other's vocal expression of ecstasy. They made love as if suspended in a creation of their own making until seemingly time itself had stopped.

The following morning, Paris seemed a much happier and brighter place for Sal and René. At last, spring had come for them. They walked arm in arm along the Boulevard St. Germain and noticed every nuance that springtime in Paris brings forth. In particular, they lingered at the oldest church in Paris; neither of them was religious but the church fascinated them for reasons yet unknown. Sal's concerns were momentarily put on hold. The day belonged to them without worrying about the future.

René was set on nursing Sal back to health while helping him to integrate back into civilian life. She ushered Sal into men's clothing shops where he could shed his military-issued, ill-fitting uniform and exchange it for clothing that would see him into the future, whatever that would be. Sal tried on his new clothes without hesitation, as he knew that however uncertain his life was to be, uniforms would no longer be a part of it. By the end of his first week with her, René had transformed the exterior of the man she loved and had welcomed home. At first, Sal was uncomfortable wearing clothes that were not part of a uniform. Over the years he had become accustomed to squaring his belt, checking the creases in his trousers, and making sure that his tie did not reach below his beltline.

"Look in the mirror. You're very dapper." Sal looked at his reflection. It did not seem to belong to him.

Soon, however, it was time to address the heart of the man with whom she was certain to spend the rest of her life. Sal, well fed and somewhat more at ease, René thought he was ready to accept a new challenge.

At the Café Faubourg, the center of many of their momentous decisions, Sal and René sat and discussed his future; in reality, it was their future.

"You can't imagine how happy I am to have you here with me." René started from an obvious position. "In no time, you will feel like your old self, again. You'll see."

"René, my 'old self' will never return. I don't want it to. You have helped me shed my old clothes for new ones, but I need to shed my past life for a new one. You, and only you, are the only thing I want to keep from the past. You have been and always will be my constant."

In her heart she knew this to be true.

"I must find something," Sal said. "I have new clothes, but nowhere to wear them. All I have known is the Legion."

"You know much more besides the Legion, Sal. You are trained in medicine." Her answer surprised her. She was beginning to grasp an idea that might help set him on a new path. However, she knew that it had to be his idea. Her vision, no matter how emergent, had to be his own.

"Yes, medicine," thought Sal: the field rooted in degrees and diplomas. "I have a certificate that's not worth the paper it is printed on outside of the Legion. As a civilian, I am not qualified to do anything medical."

Almost pleading, René wanted to infuse him with her idea. "Sal, you love medicine. I've watched you operate. I've seen the look on your face after you managed to save what was thought to be lost. Am I right? Do you remember?"

A hint of a smile struck him as he recalled his days of training at the Descartes Medical School. He fondly recalled operating with Doctor Grauwin in the revolting bunker at Dien Bien Phu. Yes, his skill, and his passion, were indeed invested in medicine. René was right. He did love it.

Sal looked away from her. No longer seeing the café or Paris itself, his mind reflected on a kaleidoscope of events that had drawn him to medicine, and ultimately, to her.

"You're right, René." He faced her and looked intently into her eyes. "I do love it. Almost as much as I love you. But, without a proper diploma, what can I do? I'm twenty-seven years old. I can't start school all over again."

René brightened. She could see the transformation in his face as he admitted his love for medicine. Her idea began to evolve. Perhaps there was a way to convert his certificate into something that would bring him satisfaction. She knew that he loved her, yet, she also knew that she would only have half of what he was unless he developed a sense of himself.

"There is someone who can help: someone who has helped you in more ways that you can imagine." René's words began to tumble at a rate that brought a smile to Sal's face.

"I can see that you're brewing something," he teased, as he held on to both of her hands. "I love you, and I never want to be without you again. So, whatever is up your sleeve, I hope that it includes both of us."

"Everything, forever, will always include both of us." She closed her eyes and took a deep breath as she could now visualize what she must do.

René made a formal appointment for Sal with Dr. Lebrun. They could have met at the café, but she wanted this meeting to be on Dr. Lebrun's terms and at the medical school. As they were about to enter Dr. Lebrun's office, the door opened as Lebrun was escorting a man into the hallway. They were conversing in a lower tone, yet what they were saying was audible to Sal and René.

"It was incredible, the work that those two were doing. I'm sure that nothing like it has ever been seen here." As Lebrun's guest turned, he immediately recognized Sal and with a sudden look of surprise, he said, "As we speak, here is the man of the hour." Sal and the visitor immediately recognized one another.

"Dr. Lebrun and I were just speaking about you! Great to see you again! You made it out!" exclaimed Bernard Fain as he rushed to grasp Sal's shoulders. Sal was also overjoyed to see Fain, who was a news correspondent, the only journalist at Dien Bien Phu.

A prominent French journalist, Fain had written much about Indochina. Most of his body of work concerned itself with the life of ordinary Vietnamese peasants. He was widely read until the war deteriorated and people became disillusioned with anything that had to do with French Indochina. By the end of the war, he had attached himself to the Legion, covering military operations that were, in his opinion, declining. His final dispatch came from the valley where, among the beleaguered men, Fain wanted to record both the bravery and futility of the last battle. In particular, he wrote about Dr. Grauwin and Sal's efforts to operate on the wounded in a bunker that was routinely bombarded.

The sight of Fain emerging from Dr. Lebrun's office puzzled Sal. Nevertheless, he was glad to see him.

"My God, the last time I saw you was in that medical bunker." Dr. Lebrun and René stepped back a little, admiring the two men who were reunited.

Turning to Dr. Lebrun, Fain said, "As I told you, it is difficult to believe what this young man did in that valley. He and Grauwin saved almost everyone they operated on."

"Not everyone." Sal noted morosely. "You know that Grauwin died on the march?"

"Yes, as did many of your comrades. I'm so sorry. But you made it out safely. I'm so happy." Again, turning to Dr. Lebrun, "This guy is simply amazing." René took Sal's arm as if to confirm the journalist's opinion.

Dr. Lebrun smiled as he grasped Sal's hands in a long-awaited greeting. "You don't have to tell me how remarkable this young man is. Welcome back, Sal." In a rare display of affection, Dr. Lebrun pulled Sal to him and kissed him on both cheeks. "Welcome home, Sal. Welcome home."

"Well, I'm off. Sal, we can catch up later, eh?" said Fain. "I know you have a bright future ahead of you, son. Did they promote you?"

"Mr. Fain, I'm no longer in the Legion."

"Well then, your future will be even brighter. You're standing exactly where you should be, at the Descartes. You're going to medical school, right? That's the perfect occupation for you, from what I've witnessed." With a slap on Sal's back, Fain left, turning once to bid Sal goodbye. "I'm sure we will meet again. Good luck."

Sal looked down and shuffled his feet. He was uncomfortable with Fain's assumption, and because he had no idea what René or Dr. Lebrun was up to.

"Come. Both of you. Come and sit." Lebrun motioned as he ushered the two into his office. "I'll get some coffee. Sal, I'm sure you missed our coffee while you were away. Dr. Aquille will join us shortly, but first, I want you and René all to myself."

Sal related his odyssey to Lebrun as best he could. He emphasized Quinn's role in his recovery and in saving his life. Unlike most of the faculty at the Descartes, Dr. Lebrun seemed genuinely interested in Quinn and what ensued since his graduation from medical school. René smiled but was slightly apprehensive as she knew that once Sal finished recounting his experiences in Indochina, Dr. Lebrun would make a proposal that would change Sal's life forever.

"So, that's it. I'm no longer in the Legion. I'm not sure about my future but," Sal took René's hand in his, "we have each other, and nothing will ever separate us again."

The old doctor nodded his head in agreement, smiled, then proceeded to outline a plan that he and Dr. Aquille had prepared to ensure that Sal would not waste his aptitude for medicine. Dr. Aquille was the chancellor of the Descartes Medical School and was quite familiar with Sal. It was he, as chief of surgery, who had been Sal's examiner during his surgical rotation. It was also Dr. Aquille who was so impressed with Sal's skill that he recommended Sal for completion of surgical training.

"Sal, would you like to continue your career in medicine?" Dr. Lebrun began.

"It's all I know. I love medicine, but what can I do outside of the Legion with a mere certificate?"

The first obstacle for Dr. Lebrun had been overcome. Sal's uncertainty would be met with a tangible plan, one upon which Lebrun and Dr. Aquille had agreed. Aquille silently entered Lebrun's office. Unseen by Sal, he stood by the door patiently waiting until his friend and collaborator gave him the opportunity to greet Sal.

"I'm sure you remember Dr. Aquille?"

Sal immediately recognized his old chief, stood up, and vigorously shook his hand.

"Happy to meet you again, sir," Sal greeted, as Aquille sat on the edge of Lebrun's desk.

René knew what was to come next. She unconsciously squeezed Sal's hand in expectation of Lebrun's announcement.

"Sal, Dr. Aquille, who is now chancellor of this school, and I have a proposition for you." Sal looked at both of his teachers intently. The palms of his hands began to sweat; René stroked them.

Dr. Lebrun continued. "How would you like to resume your medical education in order to become the doctor that you were meant to be?"

Sal's heart began to accelerate but at the same time he felt a wave of discouragement.

"Dr. Lebrun, I'm too old to start school. I have to find something that I can do realistically."

"What if I were to tell you that your attendance here would only require a year and a half of study and clinical rotations?"

Uncomprehending, Sal shook his head, all the while looking back and forth between Dr. Lebrun, then Dr. Aquille, trying to grasp what he was being told.

Then, Dr. Aquille, in his official capacity as chancellor, explained what was to be Sal's future for the next year and a half.

"I have arranged for you to be a transfer student, with enough credits in this field to allow you to complete your studies in what I believe is a reasonable amount of time. Dr. Lebrun and I have planned courses that will prepare you for the final examination for your M.D."

Sal's head began to spin.

"Transfer student? From where? The Legion? The Legion is not a school? From where did I gain credits?"

At last, René spoke up. "Let them finish, Sal. They will explain everything."

Dr. Aquille continued. "Your credits were earned in the Legion. They were accumulated in Indochina. From what I understand, your proficiency at Dien Bien Phu was comparable to most surgeons that I know."

Dr. Lebrun explained further. "Sal, as chancellor, Dr. Aquille is the sole arbiter who determines the credits with which a student is allowed to enroll. In this case, your experience in Indochina and previous training here at the Descartes have been judged to be sufficient to qualify you for admission to the medical school, and with the addition of one and a half years of clinical training, you will complete the required curriculum for a degree in medicine. Assuming, of course, you have passed your final exams."

Sal was overwhelmed. Turning to his old teachers, he asked,

"Is this real? You have enough confidence in me to do this?"

"We are confident that you will succeed, and I have the legal authority to make this happen." Dr. Aquille smiled at Sal. He was presenting a well-deserved gift to a young man who had proven himself worthy of it.

Then, Sal's old advocate sealed the bargain. "Sal, you will be a good doctor. You've been one without the proper diploma. The Descartes will make you one, officially. You have much to contribute. Dr. Aquille and I are certain of it."

René could not contain herself. She stood up and embraced

Dr. Lebrun, then Dr. Aquille, only to find herself embarrassed enough to sit back down next to Sal with an arm around his shoulder.

"René. Your young man has not yet accepted," noted Dr. Aquille, who was pleased that he could make the offer and reward someone who was so deserving.

"Well, Sal?" Dr. Lebrun asked, quite aware of what Sal's answer would be.

"Yes. Of course! I don't know what to say. I…"

"You've said it." Dr. Aquille stood up to shake Sal's hand. "I'll arrange for your file to be revised. Remember, you were once a student here. Now, you will just continue with your studies."

Before he left, René took Dr. Aquille's hand and kissed it out of gratitude. As he closed the door, Aquille turned and gave Sal one last word of confidence.

"You'll do just fine, Sal. Just fine."

9

The Proposal

Sal put on his new uniform: the short white coat of a medical student. After the proposal from Dr. Lebrun and Sal's acceptance, he and René spent a busy week gathering the books and supplies he would need for his new adventure. His pockets were full, with a portable ophthalmoscope, abridged medical dictionary, and formulary. With a stethoscope around his neck, Sal was prepared to enter the academic world of medicine.

He was quite familiar with the medical school and its curriculum. After all, he had spent over a year at the Descartes; he also remembered the attitude and arrogance of the other medical students towards him when he had been enrolled as a "special student". He hoped that their disdain for him would be a part of the past; however, at this point, he was confident enough to hold his own in an institution where rank and placement were rules of thumb. He had already earned his rank in a different institution, one in which much more was at stake. He was now a traditional student and for all they knew, he had merely transferred in from another school. Drs. Lebrun and Aquille had made it very clear to him that he would be on his own. There would be no special consideration granted toward him except for the expediting of his enrollment. Passing his final examinations would be crucial.

René quite liked her new domestic role. She, of course, would continue to be the charge nurse in the operating room, coming in frequent contact with Sal. They had both decided that their connection to each other should remain a secret, lest the other medical students suspected favoritism on her part. What they could not hide, however, was their deep and abiding love for each other. Stolen glances and subtle brushing of their hands would have to be kept to a minimum. It would be difficult, but necessary, given the environment in which they were immersed.

What little spare time they each had was spent strolling along the Boulevard Saint Germain. Each walk drew them to the oldest church in Paris, Saint Germain De Pres. There was something about that structure that gave them pause: each of them recalling the year of separation and their commitment to never let that happen, again.

Sal was in the midst of a great transition. He had jumped feet first into the Legion. Now, he would take a deep breath, and without reservation, make a commitment to the woman he loved. He was much wiser, more mature and less impulsive. No longer the impetuous youth who had acted without giving thought to consequences, Sal became more conservative in his decisions. His Legion experience coupled with medical training had taught him to be more pensive and logical. Far from the boy who had escaped New York on a ship, joined the French Foreign Legion, and had gone to war, he was now a man fully prepared for his future. He wanted to spend the rest of his life with the woman who had never wavered from supporting and loving him. He would ask René to marry him.

As the first day of summer dawned, on one of the rare days that Sal and René were free from responsibility at the Descartes, they took their usual stroll on the Boulevard Saint Germain. After buying the supplies and books he needed for school, Sal still had some of the Legion's compensation left as it was René who had bought his civilian clothes and paid for maintaining the household. On their walk, Sal stopped to buy a bouquet of flowers, not a typical thing for him to do.

"My, how romantic." René observed.

"We need flowers," Sal awkwardly replied.

Puzzled, René hooked her arm in his as they walked and reached their usual stop at the old church. There, Sal faced her, his neck muscles tightened, swallowed hard, and took a deep breath.

"Everything has happened so quickly," Sal declared in a very serious tone. René just nodded.

"You have been my constant, my reason for surviving, my everything." Another deep breath. "René, I have very little to offer you at the moment, other than my love, and total devotion. I am not the same man you were with so long ago in Paris, or in Quang Tri. But I feel that I am something more, something that you have helped me to become. René, when I think back over that terrible year, I also think about how my thoughts of you helped me to survive. I never want to be separated from you again." He awkwardly thrust the bouquet towards her. René gave a hint of amusement as she took the flowers. She knew what was coming next. She had anticipated it, and wanted it, as much as he did.

Kneeling down on one knee, Sal looked up at René and said, "René. Please marry me." The words almost burst out as Sal closed his eyes, wrinkled his brow, and yearned for her response. She looked up at the sky, then at Sal, and gave the reply that he so longed for. "Yes, of course I will! What took you so long?" Sal opened his eyes, pulled her to him, crushing the bouquet in the process, and kissed her with a fervor that they would remember for the rest of their lives.

Neither of them had a family to share the joyous news with. They wanted Dr. Lebrun to know and to perhaps even attend the civil ceremony, but they thought it prudent to keep their union a secret until Sal had completed his studies. Sal and René made an application for union at the Paris Mairie, where they signed their statement of marriage. They were told to return in two weeks' time for the ceremony to be performed by the mayor. The interval of two weeks was interminably long; even though the two were in every sense husband and wife, waiting for the official ceremony seemed intolerable.

Finally, the day of the ceremony arrived. They prepared in turn as René picked out Sal's tie and he helped her tie the bow on the back of her dress, chosen especially for the occasion. Sal stepped back to admire her. She was as radiant as the day he had first seen her. She was a vision in her soft, pink cotton dress, auburn hair let loosely about her shoulders, and the warm smile she gave to Sal as she turned to face him. To Sal, she was the most beautiful and desirable woman in the world.

"You truly are beautiful," Sal murmured, as if stunned.

"Is it better than a scrub gown?" she smiled teasing him. René had never allowed herself to regard her own beauty. She had a slight deformity in her left foot that gave her the appearance of a ballet dancer in the first position. Though barely noticeable, she avoided awareness of it to keep from feeling self-conscious about it. Sal thought she was all the more beautiful for it.

"I can't believe you're marrying me," he declared as he fumbled with the knot in his tie.

"Here, let me." René reached for his tie, but Sal smiled and backed away.

"No, no. If you touch me now, we will never leave this apartment." She laughed.

As she waited in the parlor for Sal to finish dressing, René thought about how she had been relentlessly pursued by the male residents at the hospital for all the wrong reasons. Sal was different. They had begun their relationship as friends, which evolved into good friends who understood each other perfectly. In time, they became lovers and grew to believe that no one on earth could take the other's place. And, today, after all they had been through together, and apart—They would be married.

When Sal finally announced that he was ready to go, René asked, "Can we at least hold hands until we get to the Mairie?" She laughed, teasingly.

"Yes, but no squeezing!" They practically skipped down the stairs and hailed a taxi. This day was one of the happiest that either had ever known. The exhilaration they felt was unmatched. This day would give them what they had been dreaming of for what had seemed like forever.

The ceremony was a mere formality. They stood in front of an ornate table, behind which stood the assistant mayor and his clerk. Neither was impressed by the couple they were about to marry. The mayor's designate, whose interest lay in other matters, quickly signed the document of union. René followed in turn. Sal took the pen in a quivering hand and watched as René blushed. Then, he signed, after the clerk impatiently cleared his throat. The clerk's stamp thundered as it came down upon the document signaling the ceremony's end. The designate mayor and his clerk left as soon as the seal was placed upon paper. Sal and René remained motionless, looking at each other.

"Well, we did it." Sal said with a sheepish green on his face.

"Yes, we did. Any regrets?"

"We've only been married for a minute."

René laughed. "You may kiss the bride."

"Goddamned right I may!" They kissed in a long lingering embrace that was interrupted by the clerk who returned to announce that the ceremony was over, and that they needed to make room for the next one.

Celebration of their wedding was limited to a dinner that evening at TournBride, the restaurant near their apartment on the Rue Mouffetard where they had established a Friday evening ritual. It would be the last regular meal that they would share because of Sal's long hours of study and hectic clinical schedule required of him as a medical student.

The next day Sal returned to work. He put on his white jacket while René donned her scrub dress for the first case in the operating room. No one at the Descartes was any wiser as to their relationship. Sal's fourteen to sixteen-hour days were filled with morning classes in chemistry, disease diagnosis and management; these he struggled with but coped well enough to pass. In the afternoon, the practical courses and making patient rounds in the many wards of the Descartes came naturally to him. He had an instant connection with patients who wanted not only a diagnosis but also answers as to why they had been afflicted. Sal was patient, kind, and unlike his fellow students, he did not rush from bed to bed. Instead, he patiently spoke with the unfortunates, sometimes sitting on their beds, genuinely interested in their cases. The professors of medicine took note of this unusual student, making favorable notations on his progress.

The operating theater presented students with the ultimate challenge in medicine. Ascetic and steeped in mystery, the white tiled walls and brilliant overhead lights gave way to the inner sanctum of the Descartes.

Even the dress code differentiated those who were allowed to enter from those who had no access. Donning green scrub suits and dresses gave the semblance of equality to all that worked there, but not all were equal. No other place in the hospital was as feared or revered as the operating theater. In those rooms, the mysterious art of the surgeon represented the height of healing. It was in the theater where the very real drama of life and death played a role, whose outcome could not be predicted.

In surgery, Sal was a star. Under the watchful eye of René, who tried as best she could not to show her pride, Sal unhesitatingly approached each case with confidence and skill. He had operated under the worst of circumstances in Indochina; here at the Descartes, he felt as if he were working in the finest of spaces, which in fact, he was. His skill in operating on routine cases such as appendectomies, gall bladders, and intestinal obstruction was notable; so much so, that he was often rotated to the trauma team where unstable patients were rushed to the operating theater to receive definitive, life-saving care. Trauma was Sal's specialty. When he had operated in Indochina with Dr. Grauwin, it was under dire conditions that only enhanced his skill: poor lighting, dust-filled bunkers, and surrounding explosions directly above them, permeating the air with cordite.

The trauma surgeons who supervised Sal were among the sternest academic physicians at the Descartes. Medical students and residents alike feared them most. Dour and uncompromising, the trauma surgeons worked rapidly and had little patience for students who hesitated or were reluctant to be aggressive. Sal never vacillated. He prioritized the steps needed to stabilize a patient and was often three steps ahead of the surgeon to whom he was assigned. They quickly took note of this 'transfer' student who had been thrust into their midst.

"From which training program did you transfer?" One of the surgeons inquired.

Sal had not been prepared for this question. "I worked in Indochina," he replied as he tried to think of an answer that would deflect further questioning. It did not.

"Indochina? There's a war in Indochina. What the hell were you doing there?"

"There was a war, sir. It has been over for a year or so, now."

"Well, why were you there? Do we have a medical school there?"

Sal was trapped. He wouldn't lie, but he suspected that the truth might undermine Dr. Lebrun's plan for him. "I was in the war, sir. I was a medical officer in the French Foreign Legion."

The trauma surgeon stared at Sal. Scowling, he tried to make sense of who and what this capable student was. Then, he asked the question that Sal anticipated. "The Legion? That bunch of mercenaries? You were in the Foreign Legion?"

Reluctantly, Sal replied, "Yes, sir. I was. But now I'm..."

The trauma surgeon cut him off. "Hmm. Well, no matter. I see you know what you're doing. I want you assigned to scrub in on my cases during your rotation here. I don't want to put up with these other nitwits."

Sal's perspiration gave him away, but the ice had been broken. In recruiting Sal, the trauma surgeon, as he should have, relied upon what was best for the patient. Sal's competence was paramount; Never mind the origin from which this student had been transferred. He was far ahead of his peers and he was honest.

"My name is Dr. Chalette. Put your name on the trauma call board under mine. By the way, what is your name?"

Sal was much relieved. He was too nervous to be proud; that would come later. "My name is Solomon Hecht, but everyone calls me, Sal."

"Right, Sal. Put your name on the board when I'm on call for trauma."

"Thank you, Dr. Chalette."

René observed this encounter and later in the comfort and relaxation of their apartment, while Sal was studying, she shared what she knew about Dr. Chalette.

"Dr. Chalette has quite a reputation at the Descartes. Do you know what the residents call him?" Sal, engrossed in his studies, looked up at the mention of Chalette's name.

"The residents call him 'The Dragon'. He is among the best surgeons at the hospital, but also one of the most difficult to get along with. The residents cringe at the possibility of being assigned to him."

Sal nodded but knew that Dr. Chalette would not intimidate him. He, Solomon Hecht, had operated in hell with the best.

"You're going to do well with him," René said, knowing the system as she did. "He won't be your friend, but you can be a colleague of sorts." Sal continued to read as she kissed his neck in approval. The long hours he spent studying in class and working at the hospital were to become a routine with which René knew she had to become accustomed.

After six months of grueling study, Sal was preparing for his mid-year exams. He was not worried about his evaluation on surgical technique, but he was concerned about passing the general medicine course. The professors of internal medicine were bland; therefore, Sal had to concentrate and rely on his diagnostic skills that were equally essential to his surgical expertise. One great advantage in his study routine was that he had René's professional support. Her years of clinical experience enabled her to quiz Sal and prompt him when needed. After a long day, they would sit on their sofa and René would review a chapter with him, asking pertinent questions.

"We should eat something." Sal spoke in order to distract René for at least a little while.

"We can eat after the review."

"You're a hard taskmaster. Not even a glass of wine?"

"You need your wits about you. Wine won't help," she gently admonished as she picked up the text on internal medicine.

"Let's proceed. Shall we?"

Sal nodded in acquiescence. He was starting to believe that René knew the material better than he did.

"Before we start. Can I ask you something?" Sal placed his hand on the textbook. "Why didn't you try to go on to medical school? With your experience you could have done it easily."

René smiled at him enigmatically. "Sal. Have you seen your fellow students? Have you noticed how many women are in your class? I have. One. Medicine is a man's world. Perhaps someday it will change. If it does, France will be the last to take note. I'm a nurse. My job is to help doctors and occasionally clean up their mistakes. The sun does not rise or set on the doctor. Just make sure that when you graduate, you have a good nurse standing beside you."

"If I graduate, I have a good nurse, already."

René popped the book on his head and opened it. "Yes, you certainly do. Are we ready to begin?"

With a big sigh, Sal shook his head and began the ritual that would take them late into the night.

Getting a proper amount of sleep prior to the day of the examination was impossible. Sal studied until the moment he left for the Descartes. There was silence and apprehension as the medical students filed into the auditorium, took their seats, and waited for the proctors to distribute the exam booklets. A student sitting next to Sal, upon opening the exam, cradled his head in his arms, and began to weep; not a very auspicious beginning, Sal thought to himself.

The mid-year exam covered every aspect of the curriculum, thus far: physiology, chemistry, diagnosis and disease management. Sal, with the help of René, had prepared well. He took his time, and much the same as he had been trained by the Legion, he concentrated, recalled, and wrote. Students were stunned when he was among the first to stand up, fold his examination book, and turn it in. Even the proctor was somewhat alarmed.

"Are you certain, Mr. Hecht? You have additional time if you need it."

"No. I'm quite finished. Thank you," Sal declared as he turned in his work and left the hall.

René was on duty that day; therefore, she could not meet him to celebrate. Since Sal had the morning to himself, he decided to go to the Café Faubourg to unwind. As he sat at their favorite table, sipping his coffee, he reflected over the momentous changes in his life during the past year. He was married to René, attending medical school, and, now, with the Legion behind him, wondered what the future would hold for him? Of one thing he was certain; with René beside him, he was confident that he would overcome any obstacle that stood in his way.

10

Quinn's Re-Education

The prison camp was vacant, now. The prisoners had been moved to Haiphong port for ship transport and repatriation to France. Quinn's work was confined to treating malaria as well as routine fungal infection prevalent among the remaining Viets, the cadre responsible for tormenting the now departed Legionnaires.

In the newly created country of Vietnam, the satisfaction of victory over Colonial rule had waned, shifting focus toward internal squabbling among the victorious. Suspicion was rampant, particularly concerning those who had been trained by the French regardless of their contribution to the cause of independence. Anything tainted by the French was abhorred. Quinn's relationship with Sal had not gone unnoticed by the Political officers who were trained to recognize counter- revolutionary behavior. Not long after the struggle and intensity of effort to keep the Legionnaires alive, as he had been ordered to do, Quinn was summoned to present himself to the regional chairman of the political committee to answer for his "crime" of being educated by the French.

In the capital of Hanoi, flushed with victory, the specter of retribution seeped through every newly created government department. Committees had been organized with the expressed intent of flushing out and cleansing Vietnam of foreign influences, but more importantly, to ensure that their newly won independence would be preserved. If outright execution of French collaborators was not politically correct and expedient, then their re-education would be imperative.

Quinn was driven to Hanoi, ironically by a French staff car. On his way, he was able to appreciate the stark contrast between war and peace. Farmers in the paddies harvesting rice no longer had to look to the sky searching for planes that would bomb them. Peasants repairing the road chattered among themselves, satisfied that their work would not be undone by the constant air raids that had plagued them. The countryside was calm.

When Quinn arrived in the capital, he was astonished at the re-awakened vitality of city life. Motorbikes, charcoal cooking fires, and crowded streets filled the air with a mixture of fumes and the echoing sounds of hawking food vendors. It was as if the whole city had awakened from a dream of silent gloom, which, indeed, it had. Hastily sewn national flags, brilliant red with a yellow star in the center, were on display everywhere as if citizens wanted to demonstrate their allegiance to anyone who would doubt it.

Unaccustomed to life in the city, Quinn marveled at the crowded streets. Walking in this newly created wonderland, he had to dodge pedicabs and bicycles that were hurrying by. Where had all these people been? How had this energized commerce come to be? Everywhere, shops and vegetable sellers were joyfully shouting out their wares. Quinn remembered that under French rule, there was no joy. No crowds were allowed to congregate and the only shouting that was heard were cries of despair and pain. Vietnam had risen like a Phoenix.

Arriving at the political bureau offices, Quinn marveled at the sculptured gardens surrounding the austere buildings; once pruned and kept by the Viets for the French, now, they were maintained for themselves.

The hedges interspersed with brightly colored flowerbeds belied the danger inside the building he was about to enter.

Quinn was unconcerned, quite sure that his record of service to the revolution would exonerate him from any suspicion. After all, he had provided his medical skills to the cause from the day he had returned to Vietnam from The Descartes, newly trained as a doctor by the French. His hospital at Quang Tri was well known for treating patriots wounded by the French. The skills he demonstrated during the last great battle at Dien Bien Phu had been lauded by military and Political Officers, alike. Unknown to him, it was his relationship with Sal that had come under scrutiny, as they had worked side by side in the prison camp. No matter how hard they had tried to hide it, their true bond of friendship was obvious to others in the camp.

Quinn was greeted by a tribunal of three, all in uniform, sitting behind a table on which papers had been placed by a clerk who stood at attention. Quinn was required to stand facing them during the procedure that would determine his fate. He was bewildered over the reason for his summons and completely unprepared for what was about to happen.

"Your name is Vo Ngu Quinn?" The middle officer of the three began.

"My name is Vo Ngu Quinn. I am a doctor in the Army of the Peoples Republic of Vietnam."

The inquisitor squinted thru his wire rimmed glasses as he searched for a particular document. The other two sat motionless, staring straight ahead at Quinn.

"May I inquire as to the reason for presenting myself here?" Still confident that the purpose of his presence was a debriefing of sorts, Quinn was quite comfortable as he stood at ease.

"You may not inquire. Your purpose here is only to answer our questions. You are to stand at attention."

As Quinn assumed the required posture, he began to realize that this was not an informal interview but more of an interrogation for a reason that he could not fathom. Finally, the officer found the document that he had been searching for. He leaned forward to inspect it, then slammed it down on the table.

"This is a report from your camp commandant. He among others witnessed your behavior while treating the enemy, as well as your collaboration with one of their soldiers. You are being charged with counter-revolutionary conduct."

"This is absurd. I was ordered to…"

"We are not interested in your excuses." The chief interrogator held up the report and waved it at Quinn. "This is proof of your activities. You have no defense. You are to remain silent!"

"This soldier was a medic. I was ordered by the commandant to…"

"SILENCE!" A flick of his head motioned the clerk to stand behind Quinn. The chief inked a rubber stamp, ceremoniously held it above his head, and brought it down hard on the document that sealed Quinn's fate.

"In light of your past service to the revolution, you are not sentenced to death. Rather, you are condemned to be re-educated. As a doctor, your services will be needed at the re-education camp in Vinh. Now, you may make a statement."

Quinn was shocked. He was completely unprepared for what he had just heard. He thought that his loyalty was unquestionable. He had proven himself many times. What was there to re-educate? What kind of government had this become? Shaking his head, he could only murmur, "For how long?"

"Ten years."

Quinn was now shocked by the chief interrogator's decision. He could hardly believe what he had just heard. The 'trial' had lasted five minutes and resulted in a ten-year exile of Quinn to a re-education concentration camp in the middle of who knew where. He had been prepared to resume his practice in Quang Tri. Now, the government he had served so faithfully, condemned him for an imaginary crime, that in fact, he had been ordered to do. Before he could process the proceedings any further, he was forcefully taken to a van waiting just outside the bureau office; four well-dressed men were sitting inside the vehicle. Rudely pushed into the van, the door quickly slammed behind him. Quinn was in a state of utter disbelief.

The other occupants of the van gave only their names and occupations; the pattern of expulsion became clear to Quinn. All of them had been educated by the French.

"My Do Lap. Teacher."

"Phung Ne Quong. Lawyer."

"Nguyen Van Doc. Accountant for agriculture."

The last, a woman whose hands trembled and whose lips quivered so much she could not speak.

"She is also a teacher and linguist." The other teacher spoke for her. "I'm afraid her linguistic ability will be of no further use. She hasn't spoken a word since she was sentenced."

"Do you know where we are going?" Quinn asked of no one in particular.

"We are to be interned and re-educated at Vinh. Do you know it?" replied Mr. Lap, the teacher who was more knowledgeable of their situation than the rest.

Quinn shook his head, but then remembered something.

"There was a Vinh north of Quang Tri, but I've never been there."

"It's on a bare deserted plain. Nothing at all like Quang Tri. I only know of it by reputation."

As the windowless van began to move, the obscurity underlined what the rest of their journey would be like.

The five of them, along with the other 'collaborators' were transported by bus from Hanoi down Highway One, a road built by the French, and, ironically, assisted by the engineer who was on the bus. They arrived at Vinh during the night and were ushered into barracks with a tin roof supported by four poles and no walls; they were to sleep on straw mats much the same as those which had been issued to the prisoners of Dien Bien Phu. In the morning, their ultimate insult was issued in the form of a black tunic and pants to be worn with a conical hat to protect them from the sun. Their re-education uniforms were chosen on purpose as they signified a demotion to the lowest and most basic class of Vietnamese society: the peasant.

They were abruptly awakened by loudspeakers shrieking orders at them to get into a formation facing a wooden platform in the central yard. This is where they would find out what lay in store for them.

They sat for an hour in rows of conical straw hats dressed in black, like mushrooms broiling in the hot sun. Quinn surveyed his surroundings. The earth was sandy. There were no trees to be seen and what little breeze they could feel, swept in waves and smelled of salt; Quinn suspected that the sea might be nearby.

When the sun was at its zenith, a uniformed officer wearing the red tabs of the political cadre stepped onto the platform and began to speak in a low monotone voice.

"You have been sent here to atone for your crimes. Your lives have been spared in order to provide further service to your country. What you have been taught by the imperialists, forget. Your bourgeois habits, forget. Here you will be cleansed and reborn. Labor will wash away your sins; hard labor will remind you of who you were, and what you are to become."

The seated crowd was silent. Their lives had been spared. This officer confirmed it, but what he said next provided them with little comfort.

The officer scooped up some sand, and as he spoke, allowed the grains sift through his fingers.

"You will turn this into rice, to feed your brothers and sisters who fought for you. You will irrigate this land until it becomes productive. When your daily tasks have been completed, you will be educated until you are worthy of your country. At this moment, you are nothing: You are neither a comrade nor, least of all, a citizen. You must forget who you were: No longer teacher, doctor, or any title given to you by the French imperialists who have been driven from our land. You will become a citizen, but that title must be earned, and by your toil you will become one. Until then, you will be known only by your number."

His speech droned on for two hours, listing the times they would be allowed to eat, bathe and even to speak. Punishment, including death, would be meted out for the simplest infraction such as, speaking French.

No more was Quinn a physician, a valuable commodity in this wasteland. He was to be reduced to a common denominator of the state: a field worker and referred to as number 6389. His valuable training was worthless. He had been stained by a foreign influence and in spite of what he could contribute to the welfare of his people, his skill was rejected.

That evening, after a limited meal of rice and segments of fish, Quinn was introduced to the first of many interminable speeches by the political cadre. Diatribes accused the French of polluting Vietnam and its culture. The history of resistance and victory were hailed as the ideal for which to strive. Last, but most importantly, the diatribe stressed the destruction of the class system to which most in the audience had been a "victim". Then the accused, sitting in silence, were ordered to repeat slogans of allegiance in the new catechism of the state.

"We have been tarnished by the enemy of the people," shouted their political guide. The unfortunates were prompted to repeat the slogans by radical subordinates who paced between their rows, striking those thought not to be vocally aggressive enough. A new war for Quinn was just beginning.

There was no variety or lessening of the workday that began before sunrise and ended with political haranguing that continued until well past midnight. Two meals were served daily, one at arising, the last, after their brainwashing. In the morning, each worker was issued a shovel, basket, and pick. They were marched, singing patriotic slogans as they went, to a river nearby. There, they were to dig a canal that led to the sandy plain in order to irrigate it in preparation for the construction of rice paddies. Because of his larger size, Quinn was ordered to be a pick man, loosening the soil to form the entrance of the canal. At first, the task seemed futile because the river water would seep into the opening, washing away the hard labor that had just produced it. Finally, an engineer among the "criminals" suggested beginning the canal some distance away from the banks of the river. For his suggestion, he was reprimanded by the supervising cadre for demonstrating a lack of humility, though his suggestion was readily implemented.

When two laborers died from drinking river water due to dehydration, the guard cadre set up water stations; this was done not so much out of compassion, but to ensure that work continued without interruption. As a result of working in the mud and water, the workers began to contract assorted skin infections. Quinn recognized these and knew how to prevent and treat them. As a physician, he felt it was his duty to speak with the cadre, but knowing how the engineer had been treated for recommending the canal dig, he had to formulate a strategy for approaching them.

During that evening's re-education session, each 'criminal' was asked what he had learned so far. When it was Quinn's turn, he decided to appease, yet instruct the cadre.

"6389, come forward and confess your crimes." A monotone command summoned him. Quinn stepped forward, bowed to the political instructor, then faced his group.

"I confess to my crime of class privilege." The group replied, "a crime."

"I confess to my bourgeois disposition." Again, the group agreed.

"I confess that I have watched my brothers and sisters suffer with skin infections that decreased their work efficiency." To this, the group had no reply and looked at each other puzzled. Quinn continued.

"I confess that I have withheld knowledge that would increase their productivity." Immediately, the political lecturer who was also puzzled, cried, "Stop! Explain yourself."

Here, Quinn had to circumvent his training and medical language so as not to appear like a physician.

"I confess that I have seen these infections before. I confess that I have seen how to treat and prevent them."

The instructor turned Quinn around to face him. A stern reprimand followed. "You have watched them suffer and yet you said nothing? You have information on treatment and yet you withheld it? You are indeed a criminal and need severe measures of re-education." Quinn bowed his head in submission. Although he would pay a price, he knew that he had planted a seed that would bear fruit and alleviate suffering.

The next morning, while his group marched off to work, Quinn could hear their singing as he sat, in penetrating heat, in a box in which he could neither stand nor stretch his legs, and only a daily ration of water. He would remain there for five days. At the end of his sentence, barely alive, lethargic, and unable to stand, Quinn was dragged to the commandant's hut.

On his knees, he was ordered to repeat the crime of refusing to divulge a remedy to protect the labor force.

"I command you to reject your air of superiority."

"I reject it." Quinn mumbled through his dry and cracking lips.

"Repeat it!" Quinn did so, then fainted.

He woke up in his hut, lying next to a can of warm water and a bowl of stale rice; a Political Officer standing over him.

"Do you see that your state is forgiving? Only by confessing your crimes and re-education can it lead you to being rehabilitated and reborn. Drink and eat. Tonight, comrade commandant wants to see you.

When his group returned from their day of labor and prepared for their evening lecture, Quinn got on his knees and tried to stand. No one was willing to assist him; he had been labeled a pariah. He crawled to one of the supporting posts and slowly, hand over hand, he was able to pull himself up to a standing position. The hut was silent, and all eyes of the group were on him. He took a tentative step, faltered, then took another until he was able to stumble his way to the commandant's hut.

Standing in front of the seated commandant, Quinn swayed until a guard propped him up.

"We have saved you. Be grateful and continue your confession."

"Comrade commandant I have confessed."

In a fury the commandant stood up and spat out his reply.

"I am not your comrade! I will not be your comrade until your education has been completed! Do you understand that?"

Quinn could only bow his head as an act of apology, still swaying, and held up by the guard.

Slamming his hands on the desk, the commandant continued.

"As further proof of your confession, you will tell us what you know about these infections. You will tell us how to deal with them."

Quinn's strategy had worked. He did not dare to smile or in any way appear to be the physician he was. Of course, he knew the treatment and prevention of the skin infections but was careful to relate his understanding of these to the commandant in such a manner that implied a distant memory; thus far, there was no indication that the camp officers knew he was a doctor. The commandant gave orders to obtain the necessary medication suggested by Quinn, as well as the directive to issue Vaseline to all workers whose legs and feet are regularly immersed in water.

Quinn was allowed to return to his hut. He noted that what little conversation there was among the other prisoners, none of it was directed toward him. No one in the camp knew that Quinn was the means by which their infections would be prevented or cured. Within one week of treatment, all who were infected returned to full duties and there were no further outbreaks. The camp authorities were pleased. Quinn's "confession" had worked. However, his suggestion, no matter how he presented it, cast further suspicion on him by a staff that regarded any advice from the numbers in their charge as being anti-revolutionary, regardless of the benefit

11

Escape

The docks of Haiphong were crowded with families who had hastily packed their essential belongings into large bundles, balancing them on their heads, or dragging them in carts onto waiting sampans. Children holding on to straw dolls, toys, and whatever was most precious to them clung to their parents, their eyes wide with terror. An unmistakable sense of urgency permeated the mass of desperate people pouring onto the docks that were littered with rotting vegetables, human waste, and rats that scurried in between kicking feet.

The little boats were filled beyond capacity, tilting precariously ever so closely to the sea as more and more people attempted to board. Unscrupulous boat agents snatched and eagerly counted the money offered to them. Groups were then assigned to the fragile sampans according to who paid the most. Families who could afford additional monies were sent to larger more stable craft that could accommodate them. Those who had the minimum fare, bargained with the agents and were relegated to open boats that offered no shelter from the sun or sea.

Those unfortunates who could not afford the price of passage were pushed aside, wailing at their misfortune; cries of desperation echoed throughout the waterfront. Some of the poor held out their screaming children to those fortunate enough to gain passage, hoping that their children at least might reach safety. The chaos on the docks was purposely ignored by the North Vietnamese authorities who were nowhere to be seen. Customs officials who normally extorted whatever they could from arriving and departing passengers, conveniently took the day off.

Thousands of Catholics from the North Vietnam were migrating to the South by way of a secret operation, a flotilla organized by the United States. North Vietnam turned a blind eye to the Catholic "escape" as the government was more than willing to rid themselves of those whom they perceived to have an allegiance to the church. The Viets had no patience for any religious entity: their state was the party, and the party was communist. Good riddance to a population that could not be trusted.

After the peace agreement was signed in Geneva, the United States wanted to guarantee that Southeast Asia would not fall into the hands of the communists, so a strategy was designed to democratize South Vietnam, and re-build that country in its own image. The newly created state that had been created by the Geneva Agreement was to become a free, democratic, "little America." Now, there were two Vietnams - Communist North Vietnam and in the South, a state supported by the United States.

The Catholics migrating and fleeing to the South were largely a French-educated class and, although in the minority, formed the heart of a government in a South Vietnam chiefly populated by Buddhists. What the communists in the North had tried so hard to eradicate by throwing out the French, was alive, and would thrive in the South.

Quinn knew that he would not survive the perils of re-education. Although his scheme had eased the suffering of his fellow inmates, he was a marked man. He held favor neither with the political cadre nor with his neighbors who wanted their freedom. He knew that they would not hesitate to sacrifice him in order to gain it. Fully aware of the mass migration to the South, Quinn, though not a Catholic, felt that his best chances at survival were to go south. Escape from the camp was as dangerous as remaining there, but he had no other option. To remain, and resist indoctrination, meant a slow humiliating death.

The workers on the canal resembled human ants as they dug, shoveling and depositing the soil on its banks. The further the canal made its way to the sandy plain, the more it began to cave in because of the unstable soil. For every shovelful of soil scooped out, two would collapse into the dig making further progress impossible. Frustrated by the slowdown, camp authorities had to ignore their policy of not recognizing inmates and their previous training. The political officers knew full well who the engineer among the inmates was; he had identified himself at the beginning of the project. Unfortunately, his skill, although necessary at the moment, would ultimately doom him as being impenitent, and once the canal had been completed, he would no longer be of use to the state. The commandant politely conferred with him, and implemented his engineering plans to stabilize the soil.

The river emptied into the sea, and at the mouth there was a bed of smooth stones ideally suited to make a wall. The stones, the engineer reasoned, could be used to line the wall of the canal in order to prevent its collapsing. Inmates were divided into two work parties: one to dig, the other, to collect and carry stones to the work site. Quinn was selected to haul the stones so large and heavy that only one could be carried at a time. Transporting of stones was the worst of two evils. However, no matter the back-breaking work, traveling back and forth to the mouth of the river gave Quinn the opportunity to survey the surrounding countryside as well as to devise a plan for escape.

The vast expanse of the beach was beautiful. Clear, white sand caressed the South China Sea with a calmness that undermined the political turmoil on land. However, this serenity provided little opportunity for Quinn's concealment during an escape attempt. Treeless, barren and reflecting the sun, a lone man making his way south would be immediately seen and captured. It became clear to Quinn that the only possible avenue of escape would be the sea.

Surveying the sea, Quinn saw sampans, hundreds of them heading south. Perhaps, if he swam out to reach them, he could be picked up and make his way south as well. The building of the canal, with the aid of the stone wall reinforcement, was rapidly coming to completion. In a few days, he would be forced to begin building dams for rice paddies and his trips to the sea would be over.

The next morning while on the beach, Quinn selected a particularly large flat stone, difficult and awkward to carry. He lagged behind the other inmates who were returning to the canal. An impatient guard challenged him.

"Move along! You are too far behind."

"Sir, this flat stone is heavy, but it will be needed to finish the canal. There are others there," Quinn pointed to a cache of large flat stones. "See, there. They are heavy, but I can get them. It will just take me a little longer to bring them back."

The guard had already turned his back on Quinn and trudged on to escort the main group of returning prisoners.

"Well, hurry and catch up as quickly as you can."

Within moments the guard was out of sight. It would be at least a half-hour before the contingent returned; if Quinn was not missed, he had some time. Dropping the stone, rolling up his trousers, Quinn ran to the sea, and began to swim. Just as the day before, sampans were in the distance slowly making their way south. When he was a few yards offshore, Quinn took off his conical straw hat, and threw it onto the water; it floated. Perhaps the guards would see it and think that he had drowned.

The sea was refreshing. As he swam, Quinn felt revitalized. The consequences of being caught inspired his strokes as his arms pumped and parted the sea in front of him. Every few yards, Quinn turned his head toward the beach to make sure that the guard had not returned. The beach was empty. Thus far, he had not been seen. The sampans appeared closer, forming a line as far as the eye could see: a horizon of boats. Giving no thought as to why so many sampans were there, Quinn swam on. The closest boat, a large one, was within reach. As he swam towards it, a crew member started to beat the water with a large pole, shouting curses at Quinn and pushing him away. Quinn encountered the same hostility as he tried to reach a second, then a third sampan. It was obvious, these boats would not allow him to board. Again, he turned to look at the shore; it was still empty. If only he could be taken aboard one of these boats, he might escape.

Suddenly, while treading water, he heard a splash followed by a scream. Something had fallen overboard from one of the smaller boats. Then, he saw arms flailing in the water; on the boat a woman was screaming and beating her chest. The boat was drifting away from whomever was appearing, then disappearing in the water. Quinn swam quickly and reached a child that was coughing and gasping for breath while struggling to remain afloat. He grasped the little girl and held her above water while waving to the sampan still pulling away. The woman on board, still shrieking, was now pummeling a man at the helm, begging him to turn around. At last, Quinn saw the ribbed sail lowered and the sampan stilled in the water.

"I have you. They're waiting for us," Quinn said softly as he comforted the child between breaths. He began to stroke his way to the boat, holding the child under one arm while pulling at the water with the other. When he reached the sampan, the woman's shouting calmed into sobbing as she bent over and stretched out her arms for her daughter. As Quinn raised the child into its mother's waiting arms, he saw the sail being hoisted. The woman clutching her child began to scream again, venting her rage on a crewman at the helm.

"You cannot leave this man! Help him! Help him aboard!"

As the boat began to slowly pull away, the woman put her child down, grabbed a pole and aimed it at Quinn. The helmsman's shouting at the woman had no effect as Quinn seized the pole and, hand over hand, finally reached the boat. As he tried to climb aboard, the helmsman tried to pry Quinn's fingers off the side of the boat but was met with a fury of slaps by the woman who was intent on saving Quinn. The crew member finally gave up and instead of trying to fend Quinn off, he reached down and helped him to board.

The woman whose daughter he saved began bowing to Quinn, muttering, and offering her gratitude. The breeze caught the sail and the boat resumed its journey southward. Quinn stared at the beach where not long before he had been held captive. No longer was the beach serene and quiet. A squad of guards was running up and down the shoreline searching for him. One of them waded into the water and picked up the soaked conical hat. The other guards surrounded him, each inspecting the hat, then pointing to the sampans in the distance. Quinn could see them arguing and shaking their heads as if to refute the idea that he could have swum that distance. As the sampan caught the wind and picked up speed, the last thing Quinn saw was a guard carrying the hat toward the camp; the guards were certain he had drowned and the evidence was in the hands of the sentinel whose responsibility it was to watch over the stone gatherers.

Over the next three days, Quinn and his fellow passengers were at the mercy of the wind, drinking water and rationing what little food they had. With the exception of the woman whose child he had saved, the other passengers were resentful over an additional mouth to feed; Quinn had to be on guard against being thrown overboard either by the crew or angry passengers who had paid to be transported.

None of the boats in the sampan fleet dared to dock prior to their destination in Saigon fearing an unknown political situation. Saigon was safe; this they knew for certain. Just where South Vietnam's boundary extended was yet unknown. The division between the North and South had been manipulated by foreign powers, however, maps had not yet reached either.

Freed from his suffering, Quinn began to shed his prisoner identity and, although he had nothing else but the clothes on his back, he sought to recover his individuality and dignity. He did so by recovering his memory, long repressed by the actions of the camp Political Officers. Their mission had been to sanitize those who "were" and create those who "will be". During the long days at sea, trying to fend off the sun and preserve what little water he was allowed to share with the woman and her child, Quinn visualized his previous life. This was made easier by the slow, almost hypnotic rocking motion of the boat.

Of his childhood he remembered little. His years of life in France and medical school had transformed him from being a peasant to an intellectual and a professional. He had become neither Vietnamese, nor French. Perhaps, this was the reason the North had tried so hard to erase what he had become. Yet, in spite of what his countrymen had tried to do to him, he had an affinity for this land and its people. The true essence of what he was lay in his profession; a physician. Not only was he a doctor, but one trained in the West, armed with knowledge that could help those less fortunate. Infused with the true spirit of medicine, he sought not to separate what he had been taught from the temptation of isolating himself into a particular class.

Upon returning to Vietnam, without hesitation, he treated all who came to him equally. When his country went to war with France, the country to which he owed his transformation, he remained steadfastly loyal to Vietnam. He excluded politics from his mission. His allegiance was to his profession.

Quinn was awakened by the altered motion of the boat, his awareness focused on his present state. Looking at himself, he saw the physical changes in his external appearance. He had become gaunt and worn. The hands that had once deftly examined his patients were now calloused. His physique, once robust, was now skeletal and weak. He began to take inventory of what he was physically and spiritually. He wondered whether or not he had the courage to regain purpose in a life that had been suspended.

Quinn surveyed his surroundings. He was in a boat filled with refugees who, if they survived, were heading to an unknown future. If the sun, thirst, and malnutrition did not kill him, did he have the capacity to create a new beginning for himself? Would he have to transform himself into someone he was not? Did he have the willpower to resist a fate in which he could not invest himself? All of these questions and more tormented him, but they made the voyage he was on purposeful. Time on this vessel was better spent considering who and what he was to become, rather than focusing on the discomfort of thirst and his present circumstances: this was a voyage of self-examination.

By the end of the third day, when the only water left was beneath the boat and patience among the passengers had reached a critical low, the sampan entered the Saigon River. It wound its way through marshes and mangroves until finally, in the darkness, the boat bumped into a dock. It had maneuvered itself in between hundreds of other sampans that had migrated from the North, seeking the same safe harbor. Quinn had arrived in Saigon, and in the South, where he was safe for the time being.

12

Legionnaire to Surgeon

Dr. Chalette liked Sal. He admired the fact that he could not intimidate his protégé even during surgical procedures that required intense concentration and manipulation of multiple tasks. He also enjoyed the company of one who had entered his arena by some alternate pathway, although he was not quite sure of Sal's history. During the time in between surgical cases, they retired to the surgeon's lounge where Chalette asked Sal many questions; in particular, he queried the young medical student about Dr. Grauwin, the surgeon whom Sal had assisted during the battle of Dien Bien Phu. Chalette and Grauwin had been colleagues until Grauwin left abruptly to join the Legion. Sal was one of the few medical students privileged enough to be allowed in the lounge; a promising student and under the protection of Chalette's prestige, he was introduced to other surgeons on the Descartes staff.

The best kept secret at the Descartes was the marriage between René and Sal. Difficult as it was in the hospital, the life of a medical student and a nurse presented additional obstacles to the newlyweds. Sal's schedule was erratic and required days and nights with long hours spent on the wards. René worked a regular schedule during the day and, as his wife, provided comfort for Sal during the hours that he could be with her. Early on in their relationship they yearned to be reunited; now, they longed to have time together without the stresses of student life. While in the hospital, he saw René frequently, particularly in the operating room, but he had to be satisfied with her cryptic smile.

Unlike the experience he had endured during his first enrollment at the Descartes, the other medical students now accepted Sal and regarded him as a fellow classmate, though they knew little of his past experiences. Even so, Sal kept a discrete distance between himself and his classmates because of René. She had remained a desirable target for residents who regarded her poise and beauty as an elusive conquest.

"How was Dr. Grauwin the last time you saw him?" Dr. Chalette asked Sal during a break between surgeries.

"You knew him, Dr. Chalette?"

"Yes, he was a dear friend and colleague. Then, he decided to throw his career away and go off to war."

Sal's admiration for Grauwin overcame his fear of insulting Dr. Chalette.

"He didn't throw away his career, sir. He represented all that is noble by selflessly trying to save those who sacrificed everything for France."

"What? By dying in some God-forsaken shit hole? That's not noble; it's madness." Sal could tell that Chalette was becoming agitated by the conversation. He knew nothing of Chalette's politics or his views about service in the Legion. In spite of Chalette's comments thus far, Sal was determined to uphold the honor of his past as well as present Chalette with an honest picture of what it was like at Dien Bien Phu, and specifically, how Dr. Grauwin represented the best of what it meant to be a doctor.

"Sir, you may not be aware of my service in the Legion. I spent nine years of my life serving France and I, like the rest of my regiment, went wherever we were sent." It was the first time that Sal had discussed his past with anyone other than Drs. Lebrun and Aquille; it occurred to him that he had nothing to be ashamed of.

"Dr. Grauwin was our regimental surgeon. Besides being our doctor, he did everything that we did. He jumped by parachute with us. He hiked the long miles under horrendous conditions with us. And when under fire, he performed surgery under unimaginable circumstances. He infused his love of medicine into me and, I owe my position here to him."

Chalette was astonished by Sal's passion. Most replies given to him by other medical students where clipped and tinged with fear. Sal was different. He spoke directly and looked Chalette in the eye; there was no fear, only the determination to defend his reputation and that of Dr. Grauwin.

"You obviously admire Dr. Grauwin. But why in Indochina? I don't understand this country's obsession with Indochina."

"Sir. We all knew that what we were doing in Indochina was for a lost cause. We also knew that it was our duty to obey our orders. We were very aware of the opinions of others in France, not only about the war, but regarding us, the Legionnaires who fought the war." Sal's passion overcame his reluctance to speak.

"We had no politics; we were all soldiers. Dr. Grauwin was not only a soldier but a doctor as well. Sir, think of how difficult it was to be in a land rejected by our politicians: a colony felt to be a lost cause and a burden to our treasury and people. We in the Legion had no choice but to do as we were ordered, and yet, we did our best. We had no support here, in France, and the enemy there outnumbered us. Yet, we still did our very best. Dr. Grauwin, your friend and associate, was magnificent. He was a credit to his profession." Sal was almost breathless when he finished. Now, he waited for Chalette's hammer to come down on him.

Softly, Chalette asked again, "How was my friend the last time you saw him?" There was a genuine sadness in his tone. Rarely, if ever, had he been so open, and perhaps, vulnerable with a subordinate.

"Dr. Grauwin, along with the rest of us, was captured. We were on a forced march through the jungle. He became quite ill with probably malaria and dysentery. I told the Viet guards that he was our doctor, but they could not have cared less; they suffered as much as we did. We had no medical attention and little water." Sal became tearful as he recalled Grauwin's final moments. "Sir, your friend died on that trail in the company of the men he served. I miss him. I still do."

Chalette remained silent for a while. He was not angry; rather, he was touched and even admired this young medical student who stood up to him. He saw that there was an added dimension to Sal, a maturity not yet acquired by the other students, and one to be respected.

"I'm sorry to hear that. I'm sorry for our loss." Then, uncharacteristically Chalette added, "I'm sorry for your loss."

René interrupted the two as she announced that the next case was ready and followed them to the scrub sink where she overheard Chalette's comments to Sal.

"You are a very unusual fellow, Sal. Let's see what you can do as the lead on this next case. I'll be your assistant."

A quiver ran over Sal; his neck began to tingle. This was a test he knew would one day come, but not this soon, and certainly not with Chalette looking over his shoulder let alone "assisting" him.

"René, what do we have for us next on the table?"

"It's a stinker doctor. Abdominal obstruction." René attempted to subdue her pride as she heard Dr. Chalette announce the plan for Sal to take the lead in surgery.

"Perfect. My boy, let's see what you can do with this one."

Abdominal obstructions were indeed unpleasant. Sal would have to open the abdomen, find the obstruction, and if the bowel was not viable, he would have to remove that section, and reattach the healthy parts. The surgery was known as "the stinker" because of the foul odor accompanying it.

Sal wondered why the fates had chosen this particular operation and, more so, why Chalette would position himself on the opposite side of the table to assist him. For the past year, Sal had assisted with general medical and trauma surgeries. He had mastered the basic principles of surgery that included exposure, hemorrhage control and above all, do no harm. He had learned to expose the part of the body sufficiently enough to visualize what needed to be done.

Chalette watched Sal as he scrubbed his hands, a little smirk twitching on his lips as he too scrubbed; then he broke into a soft whistle. Sal looked down and rolled his eyes. This indeed would be a trial; it would, however, be safe, as Chalette was there to bail him out. René flashed a smile at Sal, then averted her eyes as she held the door open for the surgeon and student to enter the theater. She would not be the circulating nurse on this case; Sal would really be on his own.

Sal and Chalette were gloved and their gowns tied by the scrub nurse. All was ready.

"Any particular side of the table?" Chalette asked while looking at the operating room staff; they knew that this student was about to be tested.

Sal took a deep breath and assumed his position on the right side of the table. Chalette nodded and placed himself on the opposite side.

"Shall we begin?" Chalette gave the staff permission to acknowledge Sal as the lead surgeon. The smell of ether indicated that anesthesia had been administered, but Sal checked with the anesthesiologist to be certain. He acknowledged Sal with a nod, giving his consent to proceed.

The patient had been prepared by the scrub nurses. A sheet covered the area to be operated on. Sal nodded and the sheet was ceremoniously removed, revealing an abdomen that looked as if it belonged to a walrus. The scrub nurse looked at Sal and then smiled beneath her mask, clearing her throat as she did so. Sal began to realize that this was a set up.

"Well, this is a big one isn't it?" Chalette announced as if he were the ring master in a circus.

"Please focus the lights." Sal ordered politely as he pointed to where the light should be. To the circulating nurse he gave further instructions. "We will need some large abdominal retractors for this one." Taking another breath, he chanced to make a confident remark. "It's going to be like digging a mine shaft." He palpated the belly with both hands as if he were shaping mud. Then, he found the area he was looking for; it was hard and shaped like a sausage.

"Scalpel." Sal reached out his right hand as the instrument was delicately placed in his palm. As if holding a feather, Sal made an incision vertically on the belly. A trickle of blood was blotted by Chalette. Another incision, again a blot. Some vessels had been deftly tied off by Sal before the knife would cut them.

"Retractor." Sal took the instrument and handed it to Chalette without hesitation. The operating room staff glanced at each other quickly, taking note.

Layer by layer muscles were parted, some by the knife, others by Sal's fingers, until the bowel was visible. Voluminous folds of intestines were exposed, glistening and pliable as if a mountain of Jello had risen from an unknown seabed. Then, in unison, the posture of the operating team stiffened upright as the overwhelming stench of a perforated bowel reached them.

"I think we have a ruptured bowel." Sal reported to Chalette, half asking, half self-assured.

"I agree." Chalette replied as he moved the retractors, capturing some folds of the pink billows in order for Sal to have a better view.

"I'm going to 'run the bowel'; I will need some moistened towels here."

As the towels were placed where Sal indicated, he manually took the large intestine with one hand and milked it with the other. Inch after inch, foot after foot, Sal extracted the intestine and placed it on the towels; finally, he came to what he was looking for. It looked like a burst blood sausage, putrid, black and dead.

"Irrigation, please. Dr. Chalette, would you please confirm this section?"

"It looks like three feet I imagine. What do you say?"

The conversation was natural, without a hint of student-teacher angst. By now the operating room staff worked as if two senior surgeons were at the table; mystical glances and shrugs were no longer seen.

"Clamp. Another please." Instruments were briskly handed to Sal as he clamped off the section of dead bowel.

"Irrigate as I remove this please." At this point, even the anesthesiologist stood up to look over his screen; this caught Sal's attention.

"Everything all right over there?" Sal asked never averting his eyes from the operating field.

"All is well here. Just watching." The anesthesiologist craned his neck over the screen to get a better view while maintaining even pressure on the breathing bag. The smell of ether mixed with the foul odor of bowel contents permeated the room to the point that everyone's eyes began to blink and tear.

"René told you this was a stinker." Dr. Chalette noted with a sense of satisfaction, as well as expressing confidence in his nurse.

Sal removed the dead bowel that had been clamped at either end. "Perhaps we can take this out of the room and send it to pathology," Sal politely asked the circulating nurse as he handed her the basin containing the ruptured 'blood sausage', the cause of this patient's grief.

"Yes, sir." The nurse took the basin out of the room passing René who was watching through the window of the operating room.

"How's he doing?" René quietly asked the nurse.

"They might as well put him on staff now. He's the best student I've ever seen." Then off she went to pathology.

René bit her lip. She tried to stem the welling tears of pride but could not as the circulating nurse returned and with concern asked, "Are you, all right?"

"Oh, quite." "The stench is awful."

"You should be in the room. I don't know how they can concentrate." Back into the operating room the circulating nurse went.

Sal's concentration on the critical phase of the operation never wavered. While nurses at the Descartes notoriously were harsh on medical students, whom they regarded as a nuisance, the circulating nurse's demeanor was an unconscious act of approval; Chalette made a note of it.

The rest of the case was an example of control, ability, and performance. Sal knitted the two ends of the bowel together, tested for leakage, and then began to close the wound.

"May I assist you in sewing?" Chalette nonchalantly inquired.

Again, the operating room staff was surprised at Chalette's acquiescence; the master was no longer the stern, dogmatic professor; he had been converted into a colleague.

As Sal and Chalette worked quickly and silently, their hands flying, Sal was confident that the case would come to a successful end. He also had time to reflect upon his experience operating with Dr. Grauwin, underground with shells bursting above them. What a contrast that was! Those were not conditions that were controlled, safe, and antiseptic as they were here. Procedures in the bunker of Dien Bien Phu had to be invented as trauma presented itself. Sal's surgical skill was not born in the clean and controlled environment of the operating rooms of the Descartes; they were honed in conditions few physicians would ever experience. One day, when the occasion presented itself, Sal would describe to Dr. Chalette how Grauwin, his friend and colleague, performed miracles that no textbook could describe. Perhaps then, Dr. Chalette would fully appreciate Grauwin's service and maybe, the sacrifices of the men who served with him.

The anesthesiologist asked Dr. Chalette if the case was coming to conclusion; Chalette referred him to Sal who was putting the last sutures in place.

"Yes, almost finished, doctor. You can awaken the patient. I hope nausea won't be too much of a problem. Don't want his belly to open."

"I'll take care of it, Sal." The anesthesiologist replied as he realized that he had witnessed something remarkable.

After the dressing had been applied, Sal pulled off his gloves and mask, as did the rest of the staff; he caught René's eye through the window and smiled. Suddenly, he heard the clap of a hand, followed by other sounds of applause. Chalette started the acclaim which was followed by the rest of the staff. Sheepishly, Sal bent his head which was blotted dry by a nurse.

"Well done, Legionnaire." It was the first time that Dr. Chalette called him by that title. No doubt, the rest of the operating room staff knew nothing about Sal's past; now, they witnessed the rarity of a Legionnaire receiving praise from one of the Descartes' most able critics.

"Well done, my boy." Chalette put his arms around Sal's shoulders as they passed through the door behind which René watched.

"Come, let me buy you a cognac and you can tell me all about this Dien Bien Phu of yours." As they walked past René, Sal looked at her over his shoulder and raised his eyebrow while trying to suppress a grin. He was pleased, as was she.

13

Lansman

Quinn arrived in Saigon penniless, without a resource to find shelter, or a way to prove his qualifications as a physician. In stark contrast to the re-education camp and the little sampan from which he had just disembarked, Saigon was cheerful, hectic, and above all, free from the haranguing to which Quinn had been subjected.

As he made his way to the interior of the city, Quinn dodged the innumerable honking motorbikes that sped about, at times challenging each other as jousters on the narrow streets. Food was plentiful, offered by many street vendors; the scent of sesame, onions, and fried pork mixed together with charcoal fires drove Quinn to distraction. Heat in the South was oppressive compared to the North. Quinn's pace slowed to give in to the humidity that prevented any arduous endeavor. He tried as best he could to keep up with his fellow passengers, who in most instances knew where they were going. He noticed a surprising number of Westerners; a rarity in Vietnam since the end of the war.

The French in Saigon had been replaced by other Western faces; the Americans. They strolled the boulevards as if they were in Paris; even the tropical heat could not dissuade them from wearing long sleeved shirts secured with ties. These were American State Department operatives who had been sent to South Vietnam in order to advise its president and democratize the nation.

The American men in their tropical sear sucker suits and skinny black ties were seen entering in and out of government buildings and, in particular, the presidential palace located in the center of the city. In the palace they assisted the fledgling president chosen by them to organize a new government; they also feigned ignorance when presented with evidence of corruption, the pilfering of money, and aid that they had orchestrated. Their money went a long way in what they perceived to be a primitive country; they were sure that America could buy anything, and for the most part, it did. They lived in the finest villas, ate in the best French restaurants now owned by Vietnamese chefs, and had their shoes shined daily by street urchins. Life was good for the Americans trying to encourage democracy in a country that had not the least bit of interest in it.

There were other Americans in Saigon, as well. These men did not frequent restaurants, or live in villas; they wore casual clothing, traveled throughout South Vietnam and asked many questions of the people who had migrated from the North. One of them, Colonel Lansman, had secretly facilitated the departure of the flotilla from the North to the South. Lansman was a veteran U.S. intelligence officer who knew the travails of Southeast Asia better than any American in Vietnam. As soon as the ink dried on the Geneva Agreement, he had been dispatched to North Vietnam to organize the Catholic migration south. As the demarcation line was set between North and South Vietnam, Lansman began to wage a silent war against the Communists in the North on behalf of, not the South, but, the United States.

Tall, thin, and a chain smoker, he was never in a hurry. He always took the time to consider a situation and carefully weigh his options before making a decision on what action to take. During the evacuation of Catholics, Lansman towered over the Vietnamese like a shepherd leading his flock as they made their way to the docks of Haiphong. He prepared them to leave behind everything they had. In the North, as he organized the flotilla that would take Catholics to the South, Lansman was left to his own devices by the North Vietnamese who recognized that he was doing their job for them. On occasion, Lansman even coordinated with port officials who reaped a windfall by confiscating belongings left behind by the unfortunates who fled. Shrewd and observant, Lansman represented the epitome of an intelligence officer; he was equal to anyone in the North that could oppose him.

Quinn followed the woman whose daughter he had saved. She too was pushing through the teeming crowds though her intent was to re-unite with her family. When he caught up with her, he could not contain his desperation.

"May I go with you? I have no one here," he pleaded, as he grasped her arm. To emphasize his need, Quinn kneeled to play with the little girl whose life he had saved almost as if to ask the same question of her.

"I only have an auntie here. I don't know if she can help anyone else." As the woman shook her head, her daughter responded to Quinn by laughing as he tickled her. It had been quite a while since she had heard her child laugh.

"We can try. You come with us." Quinn took over the bundle that the woman was balancing on her head as the three of them melted into the milieu, and the approaching twilight of Saigon: a surrogate family, exhausted and alone.

The auntie lived behind a tire repair shop, in a narrow alley leading to two small rooms filled with the aroma of burnt rubber and the mag-nified sounds of clanging metal as tires in the workshop were turned and fitted to the numerous motorbikes in front. In truth, the auntie's rooms had been a storage area for the tire workshop, but the owner had made arrangements for her to cook for him and his worker in exchange for the sparse rooms that, by her ingenuity, she had converted into living quarters.

As Quinn and his "family" approached the old woman who was chopping vegetables, Quinn stepped back. Their meeting was accom-panied by a wailing loud enough to cause the owner of the tire shop to investigate; he was held back by Quinn who explained who they were, and where they had come from. The little girl released herself from the auntie, ran to Quinn, and pulled him forward as if to introduce him to her. When the old woman was told what Quinn had done, she hugged him, and another load of tears was unleashed.

The happy scene was interrupted by the tire mechanic as he bellowed out commands that his mealtime was not to be interrupted. They all ate together; it was the first real meal that Quinn had had in days. During the meal, the mechanic revealed that he was planning to hire another worker because of the demand for tires and repairs. All eyes turned to Quinn. "Do you have work?" The dour mechanic inquired.

What use would it be for Quinn to explain his credentials? Instead, he replied. "I have nothing but the clothes on my back." "Have you ever worked as a mechanic? Can you change tires?" "Yes, I think so." The thought of wearing his hands out changing tires was repugnant to Quinn, but, what choice did he have? "You start tomorrow." The mechanic pointed to the shop with his head and the deal was done.

That night Quinn slept in the alley on a strip of cardboard until he was awakened by the little girl who was summoning him to eat. By the time he finished his meal, he could hear the clanging and banging in the shop and he made his way down the alley to start his first day of work.

The years of examining patients with hands trained to seek out maladies, lumps, and imperfections faded into oblivion when Quinn began his work as a tire mechanic. Fingernails that had been scrupulously clean became crusted with the residue of grease and rubber. His nostrils became coated with soot and small nicks in his fingers caused further insult to hands that in a past life had sewn patients whole. Once, he had worn a white coat, now, he was fitted with an apron that proclaimed his new profession.

The noise in the shop was incessant. Metal clanging on metal, rubber being stripped from dented wheels, and a cacophony punctuated by the shouting and berating of the owner. In particular, he watched Quinn like a hawk. Quinn felt like an intern again, only this time, instead of making rounds in the pristine wards of the Descartes, he was ripping tires from frames and sealing rubber with a hot iron. For the moment, however, he was content. He had shelter, food, and work; the future would be determined by his intellect and patience.

The presidential palace in Saigon was the anthill of the capital. Provincial chiefs, generals, and favored merchants all dressed in white, crawled in and strode out, each gaining a concession in return for a piece of the South Vietnamese pie.

Colonel Lansman knew how the game was played; conspiring with the ruling class to keep an American presence among those who were on the take, all the while seeming to represent American benevolence. The Americans provided, the South Vietnamese consumed; at least, those who were in a position to do so.

Lansman coordinated the shipment of everything including material goods such as televisions, refrigerators and coveted motor scooters. Most important, he was the conveyer of money that kept the fledgling government alive; its competition with the North and winning the hearts and minds of people in the South, depended on it. North Vietnam, too, was subsidized by foreign interests that opposed the South, and by proxy, the United States. The emphasis on arms rather than television sets separated the North from the South, not only in goods, but in ideology, as well.

After the evacuation of the Catholics from the North, Lansman's access to the North was barred. He was identified as an enemy of the people and an agent of the South, as well as the United States. As an intelligence officer, he had to obtain a means of infiltrating and gathering intelligence on a regime that was dedicating itself to conquering and uniting Vietnam; the South showed no such interest in unification. As long as they were showered with money and goods, life was easy for those who controlled the power. As for the rest of the people in the South, the majority, who were peasants working the land much the same as their ancestors had; For them, life was much different.

Baked by the sun and shielded only by their conical hats made of straw, the peasants trudged through their rice fields behind indolent water buffalos; the people struggled to harvest their bountiful rice crops three times a year. These crops were taxed by provincial chiefs who paid tribute to the government after taking their share. Peasants were left with a bare sustenance. Lansman knew that eventually peasant unrest would become a major problem in the South. Already, the North was enlisting some of them to cast a net of active resistance. Teams of farmers infiltrated by their brothers from the North recruited relatives and friends to act against the government. Province officials found themselves in a dangerous position. They were pressured to reject government corruption, however, if they did, they would be found with their throats slit. Ever so slowly, Vietnam crept towards the edge of an undeclared war.

Quinn worked six days a week, sixteen hours a day. The shop owner, a Catholic, grudgingly observed Sunday as a day to be closed. On this one day off, Quinn attempted to clean himself from the grease and grime and explored Saigon on one of the shop's scooters. He rode by the river expecting to see a familiar face among the last straggling sampans to dock. He passed the presidential palace observing the ebb and flow of hangers-on and favorites of the presidential family seeking to enrich themselves.

Quinn was eventually drawn to the Rex Hotel, the tallest building in Saigon. The hotel had been a meeting ground for the French where they would spend leisurely afternoons at the café or on the rooftop with its resplendent teak bar made ridiculous by surrounding topiaries shaped like elephants. Americans now replaced the French as they gathered to drink and discuss their strategy to 'improve' Vietnam. At the Rex, Quinn noticed an unusual number of non-Asians sitting at the hotel's sidewalk café. Perhaps the setting reminded him of his days in Paris where, he too, spent many hours sitting at the café with René and Sal discussing their lives at the Descartes. That was years ago, a lifetime away. Quinn kept looking at his black, stained fingers; he realized that he was quite out of place at the Rex.

The Sunday forays became a ritual for Quinn. Each time he visited Saigon he was drawn to the Rex as if one day that place would pluck him from his current situation, enabling him to reclaim who and what he was. Quite by accident one day, it did. Colonel Lansman, along with other Americans, made the Rex Hotel his headquarters. There, he conferred with other intelligence agents who reported to him about deepening concerns over peasant unrest in the countryside. Almost none of the agents spoke Vietnamese; therefore, communicating with villagers became difficult. Some spoke Chinese reluctantly; in fact, French was almost the official language for the head of state that knew little and cared even less about his native land. However, in the countryside, provincial leaders and chiefs spoke no French. Although they were in a position to understand the reality of what was going on in their provinces, they were unable to converse with Lansman's people.

On a particular Sunday, during one of his accustomed sojourns to the Rex Hotel, Quinn's motor scooter broke down just as he came to a stop in front of the sidewalk café. Lansman and two of his agents were sitting at a table nearby and engaged in a heated discussion over the futility of obtaining any meaningful information from provincial chiefs. As Quinn squatted by his broken machine, attempting to fix it, he understood part of the conversation as the agents and their colonel alternately spoke in English and French; a code technique used by agents when conversing in public. "Colonel, it's useless. I speak with them in French and in pidgin English and they just stare at me. I'm not sure if they really don't understand me or if they're lying." Lansman scratched his head while staring at the label on his beer bottle.

Quinn had picked up some rudimentary English during his year with Sal, therefore, he noted fragments of the conversation, particularly words such as "shit" and "Goddamn." These were some of Sal's favorite epithets. He stopped working on the scooter, stood up, and slowly approached Lansman and his boys. Immediately, all three stood and assumed a defensive posture. One reached beneath his wrinkled suit coat. Bowing deferentially, Quinn stopped, and with a quiver in his voice apologized, in French. "I'm sorry. I do not mean to alarm. Perhaps, I can be of some assistance to you."

Lansman calmed his men down with a motion to be seated. The agent with his hand beneath his jacket kept it there. Not saying a word, Lansman nodded to Quinn as if giving him permission to continue. "I did not mean to pry, but I understood some frustration over language." Instinctively Lansman knew that this disheveled man covered with soot was not a peasant; his manner and choice of words spoke for him. This was an educated sort. The colonel invited Quinn to say more while at the same time, shooting a glance at the agent to remove his hand from the weapon.

"My name is Vo Quinn. Although I don't appear as such, I am a physician recently arrived from the North." Lansman, infinitely acquainted with the situation in the North, politely interrogated Quinn. "Where in the North?" "I was a physician for the army, accused of being a counter-revolutionary and sent to Hanoi. I departed from Haiphong with a group of Catholics."

For Lansman, Quinn had passed the first test. "Why were you accused? For what reason?" "I am a physician. I was trained in France at the Descartes Medical School. I speak French. That was enough to indict me. I'm sorry that my appearance is not what it should be. The only work I could find here is as a tire mechanic. I'm sorry." If Lansman's agents were not quite convinced about Quinn's story, Lansman was. He wanted to know more and motioned to the chair at the table. "Doctor Quinn, please take a chair." "Oh, I cannot sir. Not in my present state. Please allow me to meet you under different circumstances. Believe me, my appearance can be more agreeable."

Lansman agreed to meet Quinn on the following Sunday at the café in front of the Rex. After Quinn was able to start his scooter and leave, Lansman prepared to listen to his agents' objections. "I don't know, sir. This guy seems awfully fishy." "I'm not convinced about him yet, but I do know one thing: he speaks French and Vietnamese. If he's real, we need someone like him. I'm going to meet with him alone next week. Have some faith boys, the old man knows what he's doing."

Within the week, Quinn paid the auntie for his cardboard bed and was able to buy some clothes suitable enough to meet Lansman. The most difficult part of preparation for his meeting was scrubbing the soot from his hands and fingernails. On Sunday, he went to the Rex and, as promised, Lansman was there to meet him, seated at one of the café sidewalk tables. Lansman was somewhat surprised because, while Quinn's face was familiar, his demeanor had changed. Instead of the cowering grimy peasant he had met the previous week, the man that stood before him was self-assured, poised, and almost aristocratic.

What Lansman beheld was Quinn, the physician: erudite and multilingual. Ushering Quinn into a world of western comfort, Lansman stood up and offered his hand. "My name in Lansman; please, be so kind to sit." Quinn had almost forgotten the formalities of the west. He shook hands with Lansman and took a seat. "My name is Doctor Vo Quinn. How do you do?"

"Your French is excellent; trained in Paris I presume?"

"The René Descartes."

A waiter came to the table giving Quinn a condescending look, then addressing Lansman. "Something from the bar?" Quinn answered instead. He found himself in an arena in which he had not been in quite some time. "The Vietnamese gin is quite good." "May I order some for you?" Lansman nodded. "Two gins, with ice." After a slight hesitation, the waiter hurried off daring to look over his shoulder at Quinn just once. Quinn was taking a gamble. He had but a few coins left and if the bill was more than he could afford, he would be more than embarrassed.

The two of them chatted, first about Saigon, then slowly their conversation became more personal. Lansman asked Quinn about his education and eventually about his migration from the North. Quinn very candidly described the odyssey that had brought him from Dien Bien Phu to the prison camp at Cao Bang, and eventually, told him about being charged as a counterrevolutionary. Lansman, who was an expert at interrogation soon discerned that Quinn was being honest and that he was someone in whom he could confide.

"Let me be quite frank with you, Doctor Quinn. Americans have a great interest in South Vietnam, and in particular, in keeping this country democratic. We have strong opposition from the North, and I'm afraid, infiltration from the North into the South. My job here, in Saigon, is to find those who seek to undermine our efforts."

Quinn became uneasy as Lansman ordered more drinks but was put at ease when Lansman told him that the drinks and subsequent meal would be paid for by the United States government. During their meal,

Lansman perceived that Quinn was no ordinary Vietnamese; he had been betrayed by the North and lived as virtually a stranger in the South. Quite simply, Lansman concluded that Quinn had been adulterated by his exposure to the West.

Quinn, too, had made some astute observations about Lansman and the American venture in South Vietnam. He concluded that the American motives for upholding the government in the South were far from altruistic. Rather, America's presence was the extension of a war against the communists, regardless of cost.

Lansman, as part of his effort to recruit Quinn, agreed to another meeting. In good faith, Quinn accepted his offer of a stipend, freeing him from the indignity of the tire shop. The small amount of American money offered by Lansman would go a long way toward improving Quinn's life; perhaps his recruitment by the Americans would offer him some salvation.

The next meeting was held inside the Rex Hotel. Few Vietnamese except for the wait staff had ever been inside. Lansman and his team presented their proposal. He was to accompany American field agents to interview province officials, providing translation as well as some measure of judgement as to the veracity of those being interviewed. Quinn was well aware that many of the province chiefs were in the employ of North Vietnam or were satisfying the ambitions of both sides in order to maintain their power.

In exchange for his services, Quinn would be paid, but more importantly, the Americans agreed to validate his credentials as a physician. He would also be able to set up a medical practice. For Quinn, the practice of medicine was essential in order to provide care for the people, and for the Americans, his practice would provide a legitimate cover. Quinn's "re-education" was complete. He was a physician once more, only now, he had new responsibilities

14

Kimeo

Sal sat in the front row of his graduating class. Drs. Lebrun and Chalette were on the platform sitting next to the French Minister of Health who had once voted against repatriation of Legionnaires from Indochina; if he only knew who was about to receive a diploma and accept his good wishes. René was in the audience and beamed as her husband was finally recognized for his hard work.

This graduation was far different from the one where Sal received a certificate. Immediately following that ceremony, he left Paris to rejoin his unit, which was about to descend into hell. Today, Sal would receive his medical diploma. He was now, a physician—an M.D.

As he sat listening to the platitudes delivered by officials who did their duty out of a formal necessity, Sal could only think of two people: René and Quinn. René, his wife who had helped him endure the hardship of being reintroduced to life, comforting him, and loving him above all else. Quinn, his friend who had saved his life; Wondering if he was still alive, and if he was, where was he? Would he ever see him again? If he knew Sal was about to graduate from medical school, how proud he would be.

Sal's private reverie was interrupted when he heard his name called. He stood up, ascended the steps to the platform and faced the Minister of Health who extended his hand. Instead of handing the diploma to Sal, the minister turned to Drs. Lebrun and Chalette. They each grasped one side of the coveted credential, stepped forward, and together they presented it to Sal.

"I'm proud of you, my boy," said Lebrun. Sal's old mentor had tears welling in his ancient eyes. "Good job," said Chalette. "I know your story, and this is a fitting conclusion." Chalette uncharacteristically grasped Sal's shoulders and kissed him on each cheek.

Sal smiled, "You're getting soft in your old age, Dr. Chalette." "No doctor, you're getting what you deserve." Sal momentarily was stunned. Chalette had acknowledged Sal's title; it was the first time that the word "doctor" resonated.

Until now, Sal had been consumed by working long hours, presenting cases, and finally, taking his final exams. At last, he could take a breath; he was a doctor. He turned his head to find René in the crowd; she deserved the diploma as much as he did. René probably knew as much as he; she could have done what he did but chose to support him. In the midst of this honor, and flushed with pride, Sal could not forget how much he loved his wife.

The reception after the ceremony was more like a job fair. Graduates mingled with notable physicians who owned large clinics and were always on the hunt for bright new prospects. Dr. Chalette himself had offered Sal a position at the Descartes, but it was declined. "I didn't think you'd want to work here," Chalette smiled at his prized pupil. "You've always been a man of restless adventure. René, take care of this young man. He has a bright future ahead of him."

René blushed. At that moment, she knew that both Chalette and Lebrun had been aware of the marriage. Sal nervously looked at his feet realizing that both of his mentors had silently supported him and René, as a couple. The thought that these two men who had so much faith in him, secretly approved of his private life, elevated René beyond belief in Sal's mind. She was as much a part of him now as she had been at

Dien Bien Phu. Now that school was over, he knew that they would be inseparable.

Recognition by Drs. Lebrun and Chalette made Sal a popular prospect among the senior physicians at the graduation reception. Many of them introduced themselves to Sal and presented their cards should he be interested in applying to their clinic or hospital. Politely, Sal took their cards, but he and René both knew that his destiny in medicine lay somewhere else. Many times, during his last year of training, Sal and René had discussed their future once he graduated. What little spare time he had was spent on speculating where they would go, and what kind of a practice appealed to them. They knew that they were a team and that any decisions they made about their future would be the result of a mutual agreement. Their lives had been disrupted by the Foreign Legion as well as the events at Dien Bien Phu, prison camp, and repatriation. Now, they wanted to make certain that they could stay together, wherever Sal decided to practice medicine. The only question was—where?

Sal was a man without a country; his citizenship in the United States had been invalidated as a result of his joining a foreign army. By virtue of his service in the Legion he had been granted French citizenship, but he was not French, and felt no particular affinity for France. His life experiences had instilled a restlessness that he could neither comprehend nor grasp in any meaningful way in order to plan his life.

Within his soul there dwelt a wanderlust that had been sparked from the moment he left his home in New York City. The ensuing journey had taken him from academic failure, to merchant seaman, to the Foreign Legion, and now, to becoming a physician. René shared in his desire for adventure; she fed his aspiration and would go with him wherever his inclinations took him. She was a partner in every sense of their marriage; his ambitions were infectious. Together, they were a perfect match. Neither one of them was inclined to settle for luxury, a posh clinic, or lucrative practice. René was a servant of medicine and now, as a physician, Sal was the means by which she could serve.

The peace and lack of stress enjoyed by Sal and René after graduation was a welcome respite. René continued her work at the hospital, and indeed, her income was the only thing that had sustained them during Sal's medical education. But, after work, now in the little apartment on Rue Mouffetard, they each had time to consider where and what they really wanted to do. They regularly discussed the pamphlets published by relief organizations that were scattered in between medical books. Medical posts in areas of conflict were rejected. After experiencing the war in Indochina, they each sought a location free from strife as well as one where they could establish a practice out of necessity, not due to conflict.

Although France had given Sal an opportunity for a medical education, in reality, it only happened because of Dr. Lebrun's fondness for Sal and his willingness to take a chance on him. The memory of serving a country that had abandoned its army left Sal with a bitter reminiscence. He and René would not remain in France.

It was René who stumbled upon a potential location during one of her pre-operative patient interviews. The patient was a large brown man, almost Hawaiian, but not quite Polynesian. He was a delegate from the island of Truk located in the Caroline Islands in the western Pacific; he was attending a conference on fishing boundaries when his appendix burst and he was rushed to the Descartes. In pain, but stoic, he answered René's questions calmly and added, "I will tell you about my home when this is all over." The patient's engaging air of serenity fascinated René who resolved to see him after his surgery.

The next day, comfortably sitting up in his bed, the patient was delighted to see René who kept her promise to call on him. "My name is Kimeo and I am happy you came to see me." His French was halting, as if he had just learned to speak it.

"How do you do? My name is René. I think you have come to us from very far away." He smiled a broad smile and wrinkled a nose that covered half of his face. "Yes, my home is in Truk. It is in an island group in the Pacific." "Oh, Hawaii." "Oh no, much further west." "Not Polynesian?"

His smile turned into a slight frown. "Micronesian. My people were on the water long before the Hawaiians were created; probably by us!"

He laughed and proceeded to tell René about his home and its location south of Guam in the Caroline Island chain. He spoke in a rhythmic tone almost as if he was singing; René became captivated by his voice and the entrancing description of his islands surrounded by a peaceful sea. "Are you a country?" Rene politely inquired, embarrassed by her ignorance. "No, not yet. At the moment we are a trust territory of the United States. During the war, the Japanese invaded us. After the war, the U.S. decided to protect us until we can decide about choosing our government. We are a very poor people; fishing is our main resource. I'm attending a fishing boundary conference and, having my appendix removed."

René smiled at Kimeo. She wanted to spend more time with him, but she had to continue her rounds. "I have to be off, but may I bring my husband to see you? He is a doctor here, I'm sure he would love to hear about your islands." "Of course. I don't think I'm going anywhere, yet. Please have him speak slowly, my French is not the best." "His is not the best either, he's an American."

As René left, it struck her that she had described Sal as an American. It dawned on her that her husband truly was in a quandary; in a sense, he was still the product of the Legion, a wanderer unable to claim a country; for him, France was only a temporary respite.

That evening, René described Kimeo to Sal as they celebrated the end of his academic adventure. Sal was intrigued by René's description of Kimeo and curious to know more about his island home in Truk. "You should see him. His voice is unlike anything I've heard before. When he describes his home, he paints a canvas." "Well, I have time on my hands now." "Remember, speak slowly. His French is not as good as yours." "That, my love, is not saying very much."

The following morning, the first one that Sal could remember as being a time of leisure, he put on street clothes instead of his scrubs and went to see René's patient, Kimeo. Kimeo's face broke into a broad smile as soon as Sal entered the room. He waved with a flourish, "Ah, the husband arrives. Please sit with me before they throw me out of this place; I'm feeling so much better."

"My wife told me a lot about you." Pointing his finger over his head the large man exclaimed, "But did she tell you about my islands?" "Something about the Pacific?" "The jewels of the Pacific," Kimeo said proudly. "Truk Lagoon is a paradise, but not in wealth. We are a very poor people." Sal tilted his head as he looked at the man's girth. "Oh, I am large because of breadfruit. Do you know breadfruit?"

Kimeo told Sal about breadfruit and other exotic delicacies that grew on Truk. Then, he described the islands that made up the lagoon. As he spoke, Sal was as captivated as René had been by the melodic syncopation of his voice. Sal sat with him for two hours not uttering a word, instead, listening to a portrayal of where this man had come from. For his entire monologue, Kimeo was animated as if he wanted to infuse Sal with a picture of the islands; slowly, Sal was being drawn in. Then, after a pause, Kimeo's tone changed. "I'm sorry if I have taken too much of your time." "Not at all!" Sal reassured him. "You must love your homeland very much; France is so very different. It must be quite a change for you." "My islands are very poor," replied Kimeo. "We have little government, but what we do have, and what we rely upon, is fishing. Our waters and boundaries must be protected, but we have very little standing in the world. I came here to represent my people and hoped for fairness." "Did you receive it?" Sal inquired.

Kimeo sat upright in his bed, re-living the surprise and relief that he had felt when he was told that his island's boundaries would be respected. "Yes. It was remarkable that the participants at the conference actually listened to me. I am one of the few people from Truk who has ever received an education. I was schooled in Hawaii. We have beauty, we have fish, but we have very little else. A hospital like this does not exist in Truk; in the entire lagoon of thirty islands we have no doctors or nurses, such as your lovely wife. Our women give birth as they have forever, and not always successfully. We have illnesses that you in the West have never seen. I can go on, but I've taken much too much of your time."

Sal's mind began to churn. This man was intriguing, his homeland was beguiling, his incantation spellbinding. Sal began to feel the same thrill that he had when going out to sea, joining the Legion, and falling in love with René. All of these recollections tumbled through his head, forming a visceral response. His pulse quickened as he perceived the possibility of yet another adventure on his horizon. Medical school had paralyzed him because of its intensity and the focus it had required of him; it had delayed his desire to be spontaneous and zest for living.

Now, he could breathe for himself as he began to awaken from the academic rigor, a slumber that by necessity had ensnared him. He was the enthusiastic Sal of old, no longer tilting at windmills; now, he was well-armed with a skill that could see him through adversity. His wife, equally capable, was a part of his team as she had been all along. Sal was formulating a journey in his mind, one in which he would encourage René to join. Sal finally noticed that Kimeo had become silent. "I'm sorry. Your description of Truk carried me away."

The remainder of Sal's visit with Kimeo consisted of research. How does one get to Truk? Would they like to have a doctor and nurse there? What would the government require of them if he and René wanted to live and work in Truk? Kimeo answered each one of these questions with a chuckle.

"I and two others are the government. You and your wife are very welcome but, we have no facilities. You would have to build them, with our help, of course."

Sal could contain himself no longer. He invited Kimeo to their small apartment to visit before he left Paris. Perhaps, this would help René envision the adventure that he was planning. Kimeo had one more offer to make before Sal ended their visit. "We have a priest; a white man. Father Nick has been with us for a long time. He will help you, as well."

After Sal left, Kimeo smiled to himself. Not prone to getting excited, he did feel a deep sense of satisfaction. "I like this boy," he sighed to himself. "Fishing boundaries, appendix, and now, perhaps we will have a doctor and a nurse."

"Of course, we'll go!" René exclaimed as she poured more wine. She would go anywhere with Sal; she had gone everywhere with him. Sal's fantasy merged with her own; Kimeo's description had drawn her in as much as it had Sal.

After Kimeo was discharged from the hospital, Sal and René were by his side for the remainder of his time in Paris. They gleaned essential information from him as they dined and toured the city. Travel arrangements were mirrored from Kimeo's own journey. The map they found showed black specks indicating where the lagoon was located. Kimeo went so far as to offer them an official invitation.

"On behalf of our government, we welcome you. This is easy, as I am the government," Kimeo said with a broad smile. "We might find some money to help you survive. I will request some funding from our trustee, the U.S." Sal was unnerved upon hearing that the United States would play some role in their adventure until Kimeo explained the nature of Truk's relationship with the "trustee."

"We write to them and they send us money. We don't require much. I doubt if they even know where we are. They've never visited us. I suppose that government is best when it leaves people alone."

Any reservations that Sal had about fulfilling the adventure were dismissed; René was ready to pack. They accompanied Kimeo to the airport, each embracing him as he departed.

"Perhaps, I will see you soon." Kimeo hoped. As he turned to wave farewell to his new friends, the crowd of passengers boarding the plane engulfed his large frame.

Sal and René met Dr. Lebrun at the café where so many times in the past he had consoled and encouraged them. Sal proposed the journey as René advocated for it, as well. Dr. Lebrun listened pensively, occasionally nodding, and at times leaning forward as if to completely understand what the couple was asking of him.

"Well, neither of you has ever been predictable. Of course, I don't see you practicing in a customary medical setting." René was quick to ask, "Then, you approve?"

"My dear, it is not for me to approve, or disapprove. I know both of you very well. Your paths have gone in myriad directions. This one seems to be quite original."

Sal knew that his old mentor would support them; he had been steadfast and loyal.

"Do you have enough money to undertake this journey?" "We've saved some, enough I suppose to get started." On this point Sal was somewhat unsure. There would be expenses for medical supplies; Kimeo's promise of funds was a little vague. Would the United States fund a physician? Only time would tell. "I have a little sum I could give you. Call it a graduation present." Lebrun reached for his check book. "Absolutely not." Sal shook his head. "You've done so much for us. I cannot accept anything further."

"My boy, I have no children; you have been my children since the day you entered my life. I don't need money, I have everything I've ever wanted." Lebrun began to write a check. René shook her head, not in defiance but out of disbelief. Sal looked at Lebrun as the check was offered to him; he had tears in his eyes.

"Dr. Lebrun, I don't know what to say…" "Then say nothing, my boy, unless it's thank you." They both stood up and embraced as René silently sobbed because she knew that they would never see the old man again.

As they returned to the apartment, they realized that packing would be easy; there was not much to take. The money that Dr. Lebrun had given them was generous and would pay for an initial medical supply set up, complete with instruments. Sal sat down to write Kimeo; mail reached the Islands once a week. He explained that they were indeed coming. René also sat down to write to Dr. Lebrun.

"My dearest Doctor Lebrun, you have been the constant in our lives and we shall always remember your kindness. Sal is off to another adventure, and I will be by his side to help him in every way. We are aware that what lies ahead for us is unknown but, we will make our way as we always have, with the love and courage that have always sustained us. Thank you for your blessing. You will remain forever in our hearts.

Sal and René."

15

Thich Quang Duc

Quinn sat in his office at the hospital at Quang Tri; familiar surroundings, as during the French War he had been the hospital's only doctor. It was in Quang Tri that he and Sal had been reunited – Sal, the Legion medic; Quinn, the French-trained physician.

As he sat in the confines of his clinic, staring at the wobbly ceiling fan, the memories of those days comforted Quinn as he thought of Sal and René. Their kindness to him had never been forgotten. He had nourished and saved Sal in prison camp; they had never been opponents; rather, they were steadfast friends, separated by an age of immense change.

Quinn had been tasked by Lansman to establish clinics at Quang Tri and Hue to obtain information about northern incursion into the South. This was the price Quinn had to pay in return for reestablishing his credentials as a physician. Lansman had only to send one telegram to Paris, and Quinn's credentials were in his hands in just a matter of weeks.

Lansman had arranged for Quinn to be quartered next to his clinic, surroundings that were infinitely more comfortable than the bicycle tire shop alley where he had been living. Leaving his surrogate family,

particularly the little girl who had become quite fond of him, was bit-
tersweet. But, Quinn knew that his toil as a bicycle scooter mechanic
was limited; he was meant to be a physician. As he said goodbye to his
surrogate family, he invited them to come and visit him, knowing that
they never would.

After capitulation by the French and the subsequent partition of the
country, the treaty governing the division expressly forbade the North
and the South from interfering with one another. However, this was an
illusion as neither side adhered to the treaty and the North, in particular,
sought to gain an advantage in their upcoming struggle for reunification.

To make matters worse, the Catholics who had been evacuated from
the North by Colonel Lansman formed the core of government in the
South. Catholics were in the minority in the midst of a Buddhist nation,
but they had little tolerance for the needs of the peasants, let alone the
Buddhists. The conflict in Southeast Asia began to be known as the
"phony war." This was the product of a cold war in Southeast Asia and
the Americans were determined not to lose it; thus, Quinn found himself
in the middle of a situation that was predictably untenable.

Lansman knew that the North was actively recruiting peasants and
government officials in the South, especially in Quang Tri province, as
well as in the ancient imperial city of Hue. These recruits were to act as
a guerilla force when called upon to disrupt and destabilize the government in the South. As an American advisor to the government in the
South, regardless of its being mired in corruption, Lansman's duty was
to ensure that the United States had a foothold in Southeast Asia. It was
Quinn's job to discover as much information as possible regarding enemy
activity in the locations close to his clinics; his activities as a physician
provided a cover to do so.

Quinn was very much conflicted regarding his new role. He had
actively worked against the French Colonialists during the Indochina
War and now, after his country had been divided, he was confused about
the agenda and the future posed by the political regime in the South,
which was being aided and managed by the Americans. He questioned
whether one power had been substituted for another: the Americans. As

Lansman was going to make it possible for him to regain his qualifications as a physician, he decided that for the time being, he would accept the assignment: it was a debt he could not avoid and would have to pay.

Quinn was tasked to continue his work as a physician; many of the hospital staff at Quang Tri knew him well and welcomed him back. However, more importantly, he was also to investigate and root out Communist sympathizers, reporting back to Lansman: essentially, Quinn's role was to act as a spy for the American government.

The clinic in Hue provided him with equal opportunity to remain above suspicion. Hue was the jewel of the South. Within the city and its citadel lay the foundations of Vietnamese history. Politically, if Hue fell to the communists it would strengthen their claim for reunification. Quinn's clinic in Hue would provide information vital to keeping infiltrators from disrupting the balance between North and South Vietnam.

Quinn had treated wounded Vietminh soldiers at Quang Tri during the French War. He had also been the prison camp doctor at Cao Bang in the North. This fact was no secret to Tu Dau, the Quang Tri province chief. As a result, Tu Dau decided to meet with the newly arrived physician in order to assess where his allegiance lay. At the province chief's request, Quinn was invited to take tea.

The old French mansion where the governor generally held court now was the home of the South Vietnamese province chief. Quinn knew the manor well for it was here as a young boy that he had been examined by the French governor to assess his fitness to be educated in France. An entirely different inquisitor would soon examine him for a different reason.

Quinn presented himself to Tu Dau, who sat like a bloated toad behind the very desk where the French governor had questioned him. There was no doubt in Quinn's mind that this man sitting before him and slowly fanning himself was corrupt. The chief dismissed his staff and the two of them were alone in a room that signified the seat of provincial power.

"So good to see you, doctor. I don't know if you remember me from the last time you were here." A cup of tea was poured and offered.

"Would you care for some, or do you prefer something stronger." Tu Dau revealed a bottle of gin from under the desk.

"Tea will do. Thank you."

"Well, I hope you don't mind if I pour some for myself?" holding up the bottle of gin as if it were a symbol of his authority. "This is imported by the Americans; they are now our protectors. Are you sure you won't partake?"

Quinn respectfully declined. Tu Dau poured a liberal amount into his tea. Then he made the real purpose of Quinn's visit clear.

"You were born in this province, were you not?" Tu Dau sipped his gin-tea never averting his yellow-tinged, bloodshot eyes from Quinn.

"Yes, Quang Tri is my home."

"You were also educated by the French in Paris, were you not?"

"Many of us were. In my case, I was sent to medical school."

"During the war you were here in our little hospital, weren't you?"

Quinn was answering questions to which Tu Dau already knew the answers; it was a technique with which he was very familiar. The Communists were very adept at it. Quinn was puzzled. What was the chief of this province really after?

"I treated many casualties of this unfortunate war."

Tu Dau raised an eyebrow. Quinn's use of the word "unfortunate" was a clue that he would pursue.

"Really. How do you mean 'unfortunate'?"

Quinn answered in very measured terms. The chief was setting a trap; Quinn would set his own.

"Unfortunate that the French did not leave us before Geneva. Unfortunate that our country was divided after Geneva."

Tu Dau poured himself another generous cupful of 'tea'. Now he was convinced whose side Quinn was on. To insure the game was well played, Quinn added, "I was at Dien Bien Phu, and after, I was a prison camp doctor and treated the French. I am sure that you know all of this."

A smile broke out across Tu Dau's face revealing a mouthful of gold teeth. Quinn was convinced whose side this corrupt official favored.

"Yes, I know all about you. And, I am also aware that you treated some of our men during the war right under the noses of the French. We are grateful."

There it was. An admission. Quinn's first foray into spying was a success.

"Our comrades are engaged in a new war, are they not?" Quinn added for good measure. Tu Dau leaned across the desk, lowered his voice and sealed his fate.

"We are now struggling against the puppets of the Americans." Then, in a whisper, leaving his desk and approaching Quinn with an outstretched hand, "We prevailed during the last war and we shall surely win the next. Please, let's toast to a new victory."

Quinn accepted, raised his cup, "To a new victory."

Still whispering as if some unseen specter was listening to the forbidden conversation, with his arm around Quinn's shoulders the province chief dismissed the physician. "We shall be in touch. You are a valuable asset to our cause."

Thus, the interview was over. Over two cups of gin the province chief had revealed that Quang Tri Province was in the hands of the enemy. In passing, as he was led to the door, Quinn explained that his duties required monthly trips to Saigon in order to replenish medical supplies.

"Good. You can keep me informed of what the puppet government and the Americans are up to. Very good doctor. Very good."

Within the month, Quinn was sitting with Colonel Lansman at the Rex Hotel; he revealed everything that had been discussed with the province chief. Lansman was surprised, but visibly pleased.

"Wow, one month and you've given me a big fish."

Reluctantly, Quinn asked, "How will this information be used."

Lansman's smile transformed into a sneer, "Well, let's just say that the problem with the province chief will be neutralized."

Quinn looked away. There was no question that Tu Dau was corrupt, but as a physician Quinn was sworn to do no harm and Lansman's use of the word "neutralize" certainly implied harm. Lansman observed Quinn's discomfort and attempted to moderate it.

"Doctor Quinn, whatever happens next need not concern you. We have made it possible for you to practice medicine again; your people will benefit by it. By the way, I have made arrangements for the medical supplies you requested."

Quinn tacitly agreed. He was practicing again, and in areas that were much deprived of medical care. His clinics were filled with peasants neglected by the regime in the South; everything imported by the Americans, medicine in particular, remained in Saigon. Shaking his head in resignation, Quinn rationalized that his contribution toward caring for his people was essential.

Quinn's second clinic in Hue was located next to the ancient walled imperial city. Hue was considered to be one of the most beautiful cities in all of Vietnam. Even the French had not altered the historical architecture that had stood for over two thousand years. The vined medieval walls separated by three moats had protected emperors for centuries. The current emperor, an embarrassment to his country, lived in the south of France and, like the Catholic government of South Vietnam, was corrupt.

As Quinn made rounds in his Hue clinic, he could see the imperial city and considered how much his country had lost as a result of the Colonial war and the current upheaval. The historical and cultural heritage had been displaced by French occupation and now, internal conflict struck at what remained of the country's identity. In the North, the communists began to rewrite history, denying their imperial heritage, and claiming all ancient struggles as their own. In the South, the only thing that mattered was the accumulation of wealth in the hands of a few in the government by bribery, obfuscation, and collusion with the Americans that supported them. Quinn, reared as a child of colonialism but steeped and well-versed in the history of his country, could no longer recognize it. His education had been at the hands of the French and now, his profession directed by the Americans tore away the essential fibers of his identity. He had no relatives, and no friends, save for Sal and René. Quinn was a solitary stranger in the land that had reared and nurtured him.

As was the case in Quang Tri, the provincial chief of Thua Thien-Hue requested Quinn's presence in order to officially approve the clinic. It was a formality that Quinn and Colonel Lansman had eagerly anticipated. To Quinn's surprise, the province chief was Thich Quang Duc, a Buddhist priest whose headquarters was at the Tu Hieu Pagoda on the banks of the Perfume River adjacent to the imperial city.

When Quinn arrived, he was greeted by the monk sitting in much the same manner as the statue of the golden Buddha on a dais behind him. The air in the temple was thick with the sweet smell of incense. Twittering birds having free reign flew in and about the sanctuary. In stark contrast to the reception he had received in Quang Tri, this visit seemed less ominous and Quinn felt much at ease as he sat down, facing the ancient monk.

"I am pleased that you have come to see me." Thich repeated his welcome in French, English, and Vietnamese.

"Which language would you prefer?"

"It is very gracious of you to receive me. French or English would be fine." The monk raised an eyebrow and smiled.

"You are Vietnamese, are you not? I would think your native tongue would suit you."

"Venerable one, I am Vietnamese but have of late become the product of many cultures. I am not sure that I recognize my own anymore."

A novitiate brought a bowl of fruit adorned with orange blossoms and set it down between them. This indeed was different from the pilfered gin that was offered to him at Quang Tri. The monk broke out in a broad smile, then gracefully arranged the folds of his orange robe, finally resting his hands in his lap.

"Yes, this land has undergone many changes. I am old enough to have witnessed most of them. I fear there are many more to come."

The atmosphere of the temple as well as the demeanor of the monk placed Quinn even more at ease. When he was asked about his journey, Quinn related everything from his life as a youth in Quang Tri to his placement and tribulations at the medical school in Paris. Without hesitation, he told of his contribution to the war effort. He did not attempt to hide the fact that he had participated on the side of the Vietminh, but also recounted how they had treated him after the war.

"Doctor Quinn, while I have witnessed the many changes to our country, it seems as if you have lived them. What do you see as our future now?"

The crystal-clear timbre of temple bells mesmerized Quinn as he pondered the question; his spy mission was a secret that he dared not reveal even to this gentle and wise man.

"Venerable one, I see us being forced into many directions. Division of our land has not changed who we are. We are still Vietnamese, but external forces are altering our destiny."

The monk bowed his head, then with the clarity of a sage revealed to Quinn what he stood for: the revelation was in direct opposition to any aspirations or political advantages held by the Quang Tri Province Chief.

"In the North, we are captives of an ideology that compels our people to work, not in harmony with our culture, but as a machine that devours anything in its way. In the South, the majority has become a minority; greed and corruption have captured the souls of our people. I fear that neither North nor South will ever be reconciled."

Quinn, although inspired by what the monk had told him, was perplexed by what he should report to Colonel Lansman. His impression of Tu Dau left no ambiguities: the man was a traitor to the South. But what of the monk? Clearly, he had no respect for the regime in the South, but his argument was patriotic. Would Lansman be able to differentiate between the two?

The monk stood, pressed his palms together and smiled at Quinn. "You will do much to help our people in Hue. I hope you will come to visit me again many times."

Quinn bowed and anguished over the fact that he must protect this monk at all costs from whatever decision Lansman was to make regarding his fate.

Within a week, Quinn sat with Lansman at the Rex Hotel, reporting his conversation with the monk. His impression of Hue did not appear to convince the colonel who felt that in general, provinces in the North were subversive.

"This monk is genuine, and I am certain that you will have no trouble with him." Quinn almost pleading could see that Lansman was unmoved.

"Dr. Quinn, the monk is a Buddhist. These people are not in line with our government in Saigon." The colonel's words struck a nerve with Quinn who took exception to Lansman's use of "these people," when speaking of Buddhists. What also seemed confusing was that the intelligence chief referred to the Saigon government as "our government."

"You have made tremendous progress in a very short time. We owe you a debt." Lansman ignored Quinn's evaluation of the Hue monk and changed the subject.

"Enough business for now. Please join me for dinner. The food here is quite good; almost French, I think you'll enjoy it."

Eating dinner at the Rex was routine for the Americans who made their headquarters there; it was, however, rare for them to be seen eating with a Vietnamese. Indeed, Quinn felt very uncomfortable as he sat with Lansman while being served as he was also aware of being scrutinized by the Vietnamese waiters. The Rex was an American watering hole, a complex not unnoticed by Vietminh operatives who had infiltrated the place masquerading as dining room staff; hopeful to catch snatches of information that could be useful to them.

Lansman genuinely liked Quinn. Rarely had he come across a Vietnamese who was selfless, immune to bribery, and dedicated to his profession. During their meal, the Colonel, curious about Quinn's education, learned much about the doctor's medical career as well as his associates. Quinn, of course, could not stop talking about Sal and René and his desire to one day be reunited with them.

"Your friends seem to be very dear to you. I can't get over the fact that this Sal you speak about, is an American, and was in the French Foreign Legion of all things. What an unusual thing for an American to do."

Quinn smiled. Everything about Sal was unusual; he missed him very much.

"Where are your friends, now?"

"I wish I knew that. Perhaps in France. I really don't know."

Lansman finished his meal, a Vietnamese waiter clearing the table all the while staring Quinn.

"Well, Dr. Quinn, perhaps I can help you find them. By the time you return, I might have some news for you."

Of course, Lansman could find them, Quinn thought. After all, it only took a few weeks for him to obtain his medical credentials, he had an entire agency at his disposal. As Quinn left the Rex, he felt buoyant; perhaps Lansman will find Sal and René, it was an expectation he fervently wished would come true.

In Quang Tri, the evening that Quinn returned with his medical supplies, the province chief's manor was strangely quiet and dark. Tu Dau, sleeping in his room surrounded by empty bottles of gin strewn about, snored like a purring tiger. A man and a woman, unseen by the slumbering house staff, quietly entered the room and approached Tu Dau's bed. The man accidently kicked one of the empty bottles startling Tu Dau who sat up, blinking his eyes to focus. The last thing he would ever see was the woman grasping the few hairs he had left on his head and a long knife aiming at his throat.

16

Truk

Six hundred miles south of Guam is the Caroline Island chain and the destination to which Sal and René were now heading. The islands, thirty of them, each in sight of each other formed a lagoon encircled by dots of land, each covered by a carpet of green velvet and surrounded by an azure sea.

Kimeo waited for them daily on a dock, built by the Japanese on the island of Fefan. This island resembled a lady reclining on her side with fingers of reef stroking the sea that formed her bed: a sea that appeared to have stolen the stars, reflecting them at nightfall with every ripple approaching the shore. Palm-thatched huts were sprinkled along the beach, and below the rise that formed Fefan's waist was Kimeo's village, the chosen site where there would soon be a clinic.

The only radio operator for the whole lagoon, using a coffee grinder generator for power, had advised Kimeo that the couple was on a French freighter loaded with medical supplies that would arrive any day. While the isolation of the lagoon brought peace to its people, it also left them without the benefit of possessions deemed necessary by a modern world that few, except Kimeo, had ever seen. The islands were populated by natives who cultivated the land growing taro, breadfruit, tapioca and bananas. They fished the seas in outrigger canoes, using nets in much the same way as their ancestors. They lived a cycle of life where death was premature. Women during childbirth were especially at risk. As a result, many children were in the care of their grandmothers. The Truk Lagoon was a matriarchy where women ruled their villages and owned the land; men were deferential.

Sal and René were approaching a world unlike any they had ever experienced, which was exactly why they had chosen Truk for their new life together. Little did they anticipate, however, the adjustments in store for them.

They were at the end of an exhausting voyage taking them from Le Havre through the Panama Canal, and westward into the Pacific. The Descartes Hospital, with the urging of Sal's mentors and faculty, had decided to fund the expedition and the hospital they were to build. Few, except the Japanese, had ever laid eyes on Truk, and after the war, left the lagoon as they found it with the exception of some rudimentary docks. Life for the Micronesians had changed very little since they first arrived on Truk.

At last, Kimeo saw the freighter weaving between the islands; he called for the women who assembled on the dock and they began to sing a song of welcome in a harmony that few outside of the islands had ever heard. The women, young and old, were each bare-breasted, wearing flowers in their hair that reached down to their waists. They were wearing long sarongs and waving their arms in concert as the ship approached the dock.

René blushed as she noticed the women; it was to be the first of many surprises awaiting her. Sal, worn out by the journey, revived when he saw the natives' energy and friendliness; the musical voices greeting them were delicate and serene, blending in with the beauty of the land. Before he stepped off the gangway, Kimeo gave him a bear hug, picked him up and swung him around until he came face to face with the chanting women; it was Sal's turn to flush. As René joined him on the dock with

Kimeo, crowns made of palm and flowers were placed upon their heads as both were invited to dance in a circle formed by the women.

Neither Sal nor René were sure of the dance movements; two young girls took each of them by the hand and led them to the center of the circle, inviting them to learn the slow undulating movements of the dance. René could not stop laughing as she looked at Sal who by now was beet red, daring not to look at the girl. He stared at her feet trying to imitate the movements of her hips and legs. Kimeo, arms raised in somewhat of a blessing, entered the circle, embracing both of the friends he had not seen since the day he left Paris.

"Welcome to you both. Our people welcome you. Our islands welcome you." The women continued their singing, trailing behind Sal and René as they were led to Kimeo's hut. There, they were greeted by an exceptionally large woman clapping her hands in delight: Kimeo's mother. It was René who was the object of much attention by the women who stroked her short hair and patted her white skin. Garland upon garland was draped over her; she could not understand what they were saying but could feel the warmth of their genuine expressions of welcome.

Kimeo's mother was regarding how attentive the women were of René. "They like your wife, but they don't understand why she has short hair. Our women never cut their hair." Kimeo, standing next to his mother, whispered something into her ear; she held up her large hands, proclaimed an end to the welcome, then invited her exhausted guests inside to sit and eat.

Over a meal that seemed exotic to Sal and René, Kimeo explained the order of business. First, a home for the two would have to be built. A site had already been prepared, but René, as the "head of the family", would have to approve of it. The men of the village would help Sal build their home. Next, the hospital would have to be built.

"Our hospital will need to be built with walls stronger than our homes." Kimeo smiled because he knew that Sal had not seen cement or iron in the village. "I know what you are thinking, my friend. How will we do it?"

Sal shook his head. Every structure he had seen was made of wood and palms. "Do you have a quarry on the island?"

"Not on the island, but in the sea."

Sal was puzzled. "A quarry in the ocean?"

"Yes, my good friend, we have coral. There are reefs surrounding the island quite close to the surface; we can harvest them. When coral is touched by the air it becomes as hard as rock. Fresh coral can be placed in a form, smoothed, and, as you say in France, "Voila! Cement!"

After the meal, Kimeo took Sal to the site where the hospital was to be built. On a ledge overlooking the lagoon, Kimeo had placed stakes into a carpet of grass.

"You see, here we will make a form, fill it with coral, smooth it out, and after it dries, it will be a cement pad that we stand up and…"

"Voila! A wall!" Sal finished to Kimeo's delight.

"Yes, a wall. Then we put a form next to the one standing, and…"

"Another wall. We could even put a space for a window in the form."

Kimeo's large arm wrapped around Sal's shoulder. He was overjoyed; Sal could see the plan. He understood the building method. Kimeo had picked the right man.

Sal startled when the freighter's whistle blew, interrupting the vision of their new home overlooking the lagoon. He looked up to watch as the vessel slowly backed away from the dock. Supplies had been unloaded and a mountain of crates awaited a hospital, yet to be built. As Sal gazed at the ship gliding away, he began to realize the enormity of their decision to move to Truk; he and René were committed, there was no turning back. It would be another six months before the next ship arrived. Although they were in paradise, surrounded by serene beauty, he and René had a lot to learn about their new island community. They needed to understand the people, learn their language, and gain their trust.

Sal and Kimeo soon began the construction of the hospital. The men in the village formed a human chain between the building site and the lagoon. The harvested coral was relayed in woven palm buckets and poured into the forms. While still wet, others would smooth the mixture into what would become, as Kimeo said 'Voila,' the walls. Propping up each slab with bamboo, the next wall was prepared and so on, until four walls, complete with openings for doors and windows, stood on the site that Sal and René would call their hospital. The roof was constructed by the men using a bamboo framework, while the women wove a network of palm leaves into a solid blanket that covered the entire structure, shielding the interior from the rain and heat of the sun.

While the hospital was being built, René, with the indispensable help of Kimeo's mother, supervised the construction of the house where she and Sal would make their home. This process taught René that the people were devoted to their mission. René also marveled at the native artistry that went into her new home as she watched women weave walls, mats, and floors using every available substance the island offered.

In a few weeks when the dwelling was completed, Sal and René, holding hands, entered their new house through rows of singing villagers whose budding affection for the two made them feel truly at home. After an arduous voyage, the beauty and primeval lagoon of Truk was as rewarding as it was challenging and enigmatic; their adventure had begun.

By modern standards, the hospital had all the essentials: it was equipped with a sterilizer that had been converted to work in a fire pit so that instruments could be kept clean. Sections were created for examination rooms, a delivery room and an operating room, although without benefit of electricity. Sal and René would be working in an environment much the same as they had experienced during the war at Dien Bien Phu. In a place bereft of electricity, lamps of palm oil provided light that illuminated the hospital.

After a celebration that included singing and adorning the hospital entrance with garlands of sweet-smelling flowers, Sal and René were able to survey the needs of the islanders. The beauty of the islands masked the diseases and condition of the people; the dark side of paradise made itself evident. Obstetrics was needed to curb the appalling mortality rate of young mothers who died of post-partum infection: some as young as the age of fifteen. Tropical diseases with symptoms never seen in the modern world afflicted many who accepted them as their fate. Skin lesions and fungus mutated brown skin, creating white spots on people who were tremendously proud of their bronzed figures; to the natives, this seemed to be the worst condition of all. Easily remedied, Sal and René began to treat the "white fungus" first; it was the cure that would endear them to the people and build confidence in their care of the community.

"Oh, the white spots are terrible. Those who have it are sent away to live on the outer islands." Kimeo, shaking his head in pity, explained. René smiled and winked at Sal because the treatment was far simpler than the prospect of dealing with girls dying after giving birth; an occurrence that happened frequently.

Kimeo asked all of the villagers to line up for inspection on the day that the hospital was open for business. René recorded the condition of each villager as Sal examined them, still blushing when topless young girls presented themselves.

Those troubled by "white spots" were dabbed with an antifungal solution and told to return the next week. To the islanders, Sal and René were miracle workers because in a few weeks' time, those afflicted were cured; their skin became unblemished, saving them from exile. Soon, gifts of food and wreaths of flowers appeared on Sal's doorway; it appeared that he and René would never have to procure their meals. Curing "white spots" was equal to treating leprosy, which was also present on the outer islands.

The surgical side of Sal's practice presented some surprises that he had never encountered. Children as young as three learned how to split coconuts with a machete. Often, thumbs stood in the way of a sharp blade and off they came. If the child was brought to the hospital soon enough, Sal was able to re-attach the thumb.

René noticed that many children had protruding bellies. She knew from experience that these children were infested with intestinal worms and could easily be treated. She began making house calls and treating children in their homes; this had the added benefit of getting familiar with families, who in turn sought her out, and welcomed her.

Some conditions were a mystery to Sal, though not to the islanders who taught him how to recognize afflictions that, if left untreated, meant death. One such illness was barracuda poisoning. Barracuda, if not properly cleaned, could kill by toxic ingestion. The patient would vomit incessantly, then turn green, foam at the mouth and die. The natives could identify the cause but did not know how to treat it. If the patient was brought to him in time, Sal would insert a stomach tube and evacuate the contents of the stomach. Patient mortality depended on how quickly he or she was brought to the hospital.

Jellyfish stings could be treated by the patient's urinating on them. Some skin lesions were alleviated by a poultice made of taro root and saliva. Sal and Rene relished the learning experience.

In a few months, the couple had settled into a daily routine. The villagers had overwhelmingly accepted them. Their privacy at home had been restored, as peeking into windows by curious children ceased after the novelty of having two strangers living in their midst wore off. Sal and René, together with Kimeo's guidance, were now part of island life. Their home life became a calm existence in spite of being on-call during all hours. René, under the tutelage of Kimeo's mother, learned how to prepare meals that tasted comparable to those served in the finest French restaurants.

Obstetrics and the death of young mothers remained the chief challenge for Sal and René, who delivered babies on a daily basis. Women in Truk went into labor standing up, their mothers holding them by the waist while they stamped their feet to a rhythm dictated by their contractions. When the baby's head presented, the patient would squat until it delivered itself on a banana leaf mat, and the mother would pull on the cord until the placenta was expelled. As a result of tugging on the umbilical cord, sometimes the placenta separated and was retained in the womb; the death rate among such incidents was extremely high. The challenge for Sal and René was not only to deliver these patients but also to convince them and their mothers to bring them into the hospital, allowing for a sterile and safe delivery.

It was Kimeo who finally convinced one girl and her mother to forgo the customary method of birthing and brought them to Sal for delivery. She and her mother had been on the beach, stoically whimpering and stomping on the sand for ten hours. Kimeo first argued, then pleaded with the soon-to-be grandmother to let Sal deliver her granddaughter. Finally, the young girl was brought to the newly constructed delivery room. Sal prepared her with drapes and antiseptic. It was the first time in Truk that a girl in labor was positioned lying down on a table to give birth.

René assisted by explaining to the mother, with Kimeo's translation, everything Sal was doing, and the reason for it. By chance, the first delivery was a difficult one and required the use of forceps; this startled the mother who began to protest. René, with her usual calm influence, stroked the mother's back while Kimeo reassured her. With the use of forceps, the baby was delivered without complications. Once the cord had been cut, Sal started to give the newborn to the mother when Kimeo stopped him and explained that according to tradition in Truk, it was the grandmother who must have the first opportunity to greet the newborn. Grateful, as she cradled her new granddaughter, she smiled and nodded her head to Sal in acceptance of what she had seen. While waiting for the placenta, René explained the dangers of pulling on the umbilical cord and the necessity for keeping the delivery area as clean as possible.

The grandmother, one of the island's elders, went from villager to villager praising Sal and René, extolling what she had seen, becoming an eager proponent for "modern" obstetrics for the island. The success of this first delivery provided a much-needed breakthrough to transition away from the customary Micronesian birthing rituals toward routine safe delivery of infants in the new hospital.

Truk had its first hospital: Sal and René, its first doctor and nurse.

17

Assassination

The smoke of burning rubber filled the narrow streets of Saigon as Quinn made his way through the crowd of students protesting corruption among their leaders; they were headed to the heavily guarded presidential palace. Shouting slogans of independence and rolling burning tires in front of them, the crowd was met by the palace guard clothed, fed, and armed by the Americans. Seeing their own soldiers draped in American uniforms infuriated the throng even more until their cries and chants filled the streets of Saigon.

Saigon was being converted into 'little America' as western goods of modernity were imported daily. Televisions, refrigerators, cars, and scooters; merchandise that awed the South Vietnamese who saw the potential for owning such luxuries and, perhaps, the opportunity to change their lives: if only they had had access to them. Everything that the Americans introduced into the fledgling nation was divided between the president, his generals, and the elite circle that controlled the country. What was left over was sold on the black market at prices few could afford.

To make matters worse, the Catholic head of state, aided by his family and a church that tolerated no traditional or historical practice of worship, waged a campaign of terror against Buddhists who represented an overwhelming majority in the country. Education, government employment, and even rank in a conscripted army were limited to Catholics only.

The riots began in the universities, which were newly established after the partition of the country. Now, they had suddenly barred the students whose imagination had been fired by newfound independence. They would soon come to realize that because of their religion, they would be relegated to a life no better than the peasants who preceded them. Like their parents, they would remain impoverished while the government profited from their sweat. They were destined to work the rice fields and feed the rich. Instead of passively accepting this fate, they took to the streets and revolted.

But, once students had tasted the possibility of opportunity, their appetites would not be extinguished; they, Buddhists all, represented the majority, and they knew it. Asian stoicism and acceptance went up in the smoke that drifted towards the presidential palace.

This, then, was the situation in a city engulfed by turmoil as Quinn made his way to a meeting with Lansman at the Rex Hotel. Lansman, well on his way to becoming drunk, sat alone inside of the hotel lobby that was unusually quiet with most of the Vietnamese staff having joined the protests. A lone bartender polishing a glass, squinting his eyes to see anything of interest outside.

"Aren't you going to join them, Charlie?" Lansman asked the barkeep whose name, in fact, was not 'Charlie', but had been christened so by the Americans who gave nicknames to anything they did not understand.

"No. I am too old to stand up for another change. Another beer?"

"I'll wait, Charlie. Got work to do."

Quinn peeked inside the lobby, hesitant to enter because as a Vietnamese he still felt unnerved by entering the haunt of the Americans. Lansman saw him and laughed.

"For God's sakes, Quinn, get your ass over here. It's your own country after all."

The bartender raised his eyebrows and smirked.

"I'll have that beer now, Charlie, make it two."

Quinn sat down, looking around at the deserted lobby he placed his hands around the cold bottle and began to scrape the label off with his fingernails.

"It's very quiet here today."

"Yes, they're all out there in the streets hollering for God knows what. I just don't understand these Vietnamese, we give them everything."

Quinn stared at the bottle, perhaps Lansman had forgotten that he was sitting with a Vietnamese.

"Oh, I don't mean you, Quinn. You're not like those people in the streets. You're...."

"Civilized?" Quinn finished the sentence for Lansman who looked away somewhat embarrassed. Then, he dangled a carrot.

"I have some news about your friend, the one you asked me to inquire about."

"Sal?" Quinn alerted, sat up straight, and focused on Lansman. Before the colonel could reply, two Vietnamese monks dressed in saffron robes stood at the entrance to the hotel and began to shout. The bartender approached them just as one of the monks shrieked and threw a bowl of what looked like blood into the lobby. Lansman and Quinn stood in alarm as the monks ran off, their cries echoing behind them.

The bartender began to soak up the red liquid that was in reality paint, but the message to the hotel, inhabited by Americans, was clear.

Lansman shouted, "Goddamn it, those were Buddhists! Shit! I thought that these were student riots." He moved closer to the hotel entrance to get a quick look before returning to his table with Quinn.

The bartender mumbled as he cleaned up the mess.

"What is it, Charlie? Do you know something that I don't?"

The bartender closed his eyes and shook his head as if toward the ignorance displayed by the Americans he served.

"Out with it, Charlie. What's up?"

Quinn answered, instead. "Colonel, the demonstrators are all Buddhists, monks, students, all of them. They want their country back."

"Well shit, they have it. The French are gone, what more do they want?"

The bartender went back behind the bar and whispered something softly in Vietnamese.

"Colonel Lansman, you have sent me north to gather intelligence about guerilla activities. I have learned much about enemy activities, but I have also learned that the people are much displeased about our government. It is corrupt; Catholic, with a Buddhist nation to govern. And..." Quinn hesitated, uncertain how Lansman would react to the rest of what he had to say.

"Go ahead. I trust you, Quinn, that's why I sent you north."

"Colonel, the people believe that you Americans are partly to blame for the injustices of the government."

"That's a load of bullshit. We're giving this government everything. Training and arming their military. Giving them stuff they've never had before..."

"But it's not getting to the people."

"What?"

"All the "stuff" stays here in Saigon. Up north where you've sent me, life for the people has changed very little from when they lived under the French or the Communists. The only thing that has changed are the colors of the flags."

Lansman stood up and went to the bar. The bartender handed him another beer and shook his head. Quinn, remaining at the table, could think of nothing except the news Lansman had about Sal.

"Look, I want you to go back up north and find out if that Buddhist monk of yours in Hue is stirring things up. I've had reports that he's influential and might be behind this whole mess." Lansman slammed his bottle on the table.

Quinn, quite unused to the colonel's display of anger remained silent and guarded.

"I've been in this Goddamned country for years. Everything we've done for these people has been for their benefit and this is how they repay us? You go back up there and talk to this guy. When you come back, I'll tell you about your friend."

Quinn felt helpless; this was blackmail, and there was nothing he could do about it. He stood up, placed his half-finished bottle of beer on the table, and gave Lansman an unenthusiastic nod.

"I'll get you whatever information I can, but, please, sir, my friend..."

"All right, all right. When you get back."

Quinn left the Rex and Lansman, who by now was completely drunk. He weaved his way through the shouting melee, astonished at how large the crowd had become; this was no ordinary protest, this bordered on a rebellion.

Arriving in Hue, Quinn noticed that the city was very much subdued and strangely quiet. Unlike the crowds in Saigon, small groups of people were noiselessly moving toward to the pagoda next to the Imperial Palace; when asked where and why they were going, Quinn was met with silence. The people bowed their heads and prepared incense sticks as if a ceremony was about to take place.

He reached the pagoda, in front of which a dais had been erected surrounded by all of the monks who called the temple their home. Quinn stood among the submissive crowd, unable to make any progress towards the temple; his mission, to speak with the monk elder, thwarted by the hushed throng that refused to move. Thich Quang Duc, the monk he had previously met and with whom he had planned to speak, appeared, his eyes seeking something in the distance. He walked slowly, a procession of one, until he placed himself on the low platform and sat in a lotus position.

His appearance was a signal to the crowd who, in unison, lit their incense sticks and holding them between their palms, began rocking themselves as if the monk elder had cast a spell over them. Thich Quang Duc spoke not a word as one of the monks picked up a jerry can of gasoline and slowly poured it over him, soaking him completely. Quinn stood completely still, horrified, as another monk struck matches and dropped them onto the lap of one who had chosen to sacrifice his life for a cause well understood by the crowd, however, incomprehensible to Quinn.

With a puff, the gasoline ignited, and set the monk ablaze. Engulfed in flames, he did not stir or utter a word; quietly accepting his fate, burning until his frame crumbled into ashes. Gathered by his monks, the ashes were placed into a box as the flames that had consumed Thich Quang Duc dissolved into a sweet-scented plume of smoke.

The crowd dispersed as Quinn was finally able to make his way to the pagoda; a solitary monk stood at the entrance as if to guard the sanctity of the temple. Quinn looked at him for any sign of despair or anguish; the monk giving only the appearance of tranquil resignation.

"Can you tell me why this has happened?" Quinn almost pleadingly begged for an answer.

The monk turned his back and walked slowly into the temple.

"Wait, please! I don't understand!"

The monk turned and stared at Quinn. Clearly, he was looking at a Vietnamese and, just as certainly, the man he saw had no idea of what had just taken place.

"Please." Quinn had gotten the monk's attention.

"Thich Quang Duc is only the first. Many others will follow."

"I don't understand. Why?"

"If you don't understand, there is no reason to explain." The monk turned and made his way into the recesses of the temple; Quinn dared not follow.

Quinn spent the rest of the week in the Hue clinic, his patients feigning ignorance to his questions over what had occurred at the temple. There were no further demonstrations and, in contrast to Saigon, his stay in Hue was almost serene. He continued to wonder what information Lansman had about Sal; would they ever see each other again? One thing was certain, he could no longer be a spy in a country he no longer recognized, and one that was manipulated by the Americans; Lansman, in particular.

Upon arriving in Saigon, Quinn immediately sought out Lansman to report on what had occurred in Hue.

"What do you mean the guy set himself on fire?" Lansman asked, sitting at his usual table, this time taking notes. Surprisingly enough, 'Charlie', the bartender, had been replaced by a Chinese woman whose constant smile was frozen on her face.

"It was Thich Quang Duc, the monk you sent me to see."

"What about him?" Lansman seemed distracted, his eyes never leaving the pleasing figure of the new bartender.

"He was willingly set on fire."

That shook the colonel awake. "Are you shitting me? That guy was the head Buddhist in Hue."

"It was a protest of sorts. No one would tell me why he did it. I have the feeling that something, I don't know what, is going to happen in Hue."

Lansman furiously scribbled notes, then checked his watch and stood up. "I've got a meeting at the palace. I'll check back with you, tomorrow."

"But sir, about my friend. You said that you had some information…"

"Oh, him." Lansman said as he stood and gathered up his papers, "Yes, he and his wife are in Truk. They've built some kind of a hospital there. Look, I'll see you tomorrow. I've got to get on top of this Hue thing."

Lansman hurriedly left the lobby, got into his waiting sedan, and sped off before Quinn could ask any more questions.

Quinn remained at the table, puzzled about the scant information he had been given.

"I can bring you something?" The new bartender with the frozen grin asked. Quinn waved her off as he tried to piece together what little Lansman had told him. Sal had a wife? Surely, it must be René. A hospital? And, where was Truk? To complicate matters, as a Vietnamese, he had limited access to getting information without raising suspicion over his activities with the Americans. He would have to wait for Lansman.

Saigon was quiet. Within a week, the riots in the streets had been suppressed by the Vietnamese Army whose presence was everywhere. Armed and patrolling every street, soldiers faced the glares of a frustrated population. The students were especially frustrated because they had been barred from entering their schools until they registered with the government. They were also being required to sign a pledge to obey the will of the president. Many of them believed, and rightly so, that in reality, registration was an effort to draft them into the army.

The suicide of Thich Quang Duc disturbed Quinn to the point that he no longer chose to work in Hue. Lansman would not be pleased, but in Quinn's mind he had no choice. Aimlessly, Quinn wandered the streets of Saigon; he no longer recognized his own country. The changes that the Americans had wrought were not for the best. Previously, the country had peasants and mandarins, but now, a middle class had emerged; one that was corrupt and had no ownership in the country except for the purpose of making money. Worse still, the new class had nothing but contempt for the country people; the peasants that invested toil and sometimes their lives for the sake of feeding the populace. Avarice and power had replaced the desire to be free from communist oppression; in his heart, Quinn knew that the new South he was witnessing would not, and could not, last. The North had discipline and purpose, although harshly implemented. Quinn knew this from experience for he had been a part of that system which rejected the culture cultivated in the South. Ultimately, the North would win; even if it took years.

Quinn briefly pondered returning to the North, but his meeting with Lansman would erase any thoughts of doing so, turning him in a completely different direction.

The new bartender with the sardonic smile greeted Quinn as he entered the Rex and directed him to Lansman's table. The colonel was agitated and in a heated argument with his two subordinates, pointing, waving, and occasionally pounding his fist on the table. Quinn hesitated as he approached the group of CIA agents, maintaining a respectful distance. At last, the colonel waved the two away on an errand and motioned to Quinn.

"Quinn, sit down. Got some important stuff to discuss."

"Sir, I hope you have news of my friend."

"What? Oh, that. Yes, I'll get to that in a minute. First, I have an urgent matter to discuss with you."

The bartender slinked over delivering beer, waiting for another order."

"That's all," Lansman waving her away; her smile never leaving a face whose ears were sharp and always listening.

"Look, Quinn, we have a situation here. The president has gone rogue and something is in the works to stop him. Your people, some of the generals, are going to take matters into their own hands." Lansman paused in an attempt to draw Quinn's curiosity. Quinn merely listened, more focused on any information that the colonel could give him about Sal, and perhaps, René.

"Did you hear me? I'm going to need your help. I want you to infiltrate the Vietnamese Army Headquarters and get to that fat general, Big Minh. See what you can find out."

"But, sir, I'm a doctor. How do you suppose that I can do this?"

"Precisely. You're a doctor and have credentials. I'll give you additional papers and clearance. You'll find a way. Just say that you are there to give the fat boy a physical on behalf of the American "company." We have a dentist that will join you. Our president knows all about your people's plan. We just don't know the details. But, one thing more, you must ensure that nothing you do can be traced back to us, I mean my organization. That's most imperative."

Quinn was beginning to understand that the man in front of whom he sat was negotiating the politics of Saigon; he was more powerful than he had at first imagined. There was a coup in the works, and the Americans had given their blessing; nothing could be traced back to them. This was a level of international politics that he did not understand.

"Look. You do this thing for me and I'll tell you where your friends are. More than that, I'll arrange for you to leave this place and join them. What do you say?"

There was nothing more to say. Quinn would have to trust this man to do as he said. There was no other option.

"I'll do what I can." He acquiesced. "I hope you will keep your word about my friends."

"You're damn straight, I will. You've been a lot of help to us, Quinn;

I promise you that I'll keep my word. Now, our dentist already has an appointment with Big Minh. You'll join him and do the physical. Find out what you can and report back to me. This has been a cluster fuck and my people need to stay on top of things."

From that point on, Quinn knew that he had to leave Vietnam. He was convinced that the communists in the North would take advantage of the chaos in the South; he was also sure that eventually they would win. This was no longer a country he recognized. Thus far, he had been fortunate. He had a skill, his credentials, and the word of an extremely powerful American, but how long would his situation remain safe?

The dentist that Quinn met was extremely proud of his mouth full of gold; this alone raised suspicion that he was a man for hire. The taps on the dentist's shoes echoed in the hallway of the minister of defense. Uniformed, high-ranking soldiers walked briskly by the dentist and Quinn as they found their way to General 'Big' Minh's office. The general's receptionist, a young woman wearing a mini-skirt and white go-go boots asked them to sit until summoned. She was a perfect example of a South Vietnamese woman, traditionally modest and serene, corrupted by the infiltration of American Culture.

Big Minh sat behind a large teak desk looking impressive as he signed orders with a flourish, then handed them to his adjutant. As Quinn entered Minh's office, he noticed that the picture of the South Vietnamese president had been removed and was on the floor leaning against the wall. The dentist shook hands with the general and exchanged some pleasantries while Quinn waited patiently for the hammer to fall. Big Minh wasted no time in detailing the plan that he had for his two visitors.

"You are the doctor sent by the Americans?" Quinn nodded, but said nothing. "No doubt you both know that we are about to free this country from corruption," said, perhaps, the most corrupt member of the military. "This president has brought us into chaos, and we have decided to remove him." Minh failed to mention to whom he was referring when he said "we".

It was suddenly very clear to Quinn that the Americans, specifically

Colonel Lansman, was involved in what was about to happen. Lansman had told him to "infiltrate," but, in reality, he was mandated to be complicit in the general's plot; Minh had just acknowledged that Quinn had been 'sent by the Americans.'

"You will accompany me and some of my staff to the palace this evening. We have been invited by the president to attend a briefing. The president and his brother have great plans for my army to begin an offensive that is foolish and wasteful. I have intention of stirring a pot in which the soup is content to simmer."

Quinn had seen the simmering pot; vast amounts of American products now surging into South Vietnam, and currency lining the pockets of government leaders, including generals like Minh who were enabled by the U.S. government to maintain his lifestyle without putting himself at risk. Big Minh's eyes narrowed as he came to the point.

"The president and his brother will be eliminated. You, doctor, will certify their deaths. You," he pointed to his friend, the dentist, "will pull teeth and bring them to me for safekeeping, in case we need further proof of death."

Beads of sweat creased Quinn's forehead. What kind of plot had Lansman forced him into? Certainly, Big Minh meant business and there was no way now that Quinn could refuse or negotiate an exit; his life would be forfeited if he tried. This was no mere political machination. This was an act that could change the country; for better or, most certainly, for worse.

"Have I been clear as to your duty? Don't worry, you will be under my protection and I will take care of both of you." Big Minh reached for a crystal decanter and poured whiskey into three glasses. As Quinn's slightly trembling hand held his glass, the general toasted. "To a prosperous South Vietnam." The dentist heartily repeated the toast, Quinn mumbled his accession, and swallowed his drink.

A small convoy of jeeps awaited Quinn and the dentist when they arrived at army headquarters that evening. The soldiers accompanying them were heavily armed; Big Minh was absent, and instead, a major seemed to take command of the mission.

The group silently entered the courtyard of the presidential palace. It was almost as if the soldiers guarding the palace knew what was about to happen. They stepped aside as the general's men were allowed to enter. They encountered no resistance until the president's military aid stepped out of the reception hall door and stopped the major, demanding, "Where is General Minh!"

As he reached for the door, the major calmly reassured the aid. "He will be arriving shortly. He has the plans and maps requested by the president."

"Why are your men armed? This is most unusual. Have them wait outside," replied the aid as he stepped in front of the door in an attempt to block it.

The major pulled out his revolver and without hesitation shot the aid in the face, causing him to crumble against the door which jolted and jarred slightly open. Quinn could see the president inside, looking startled momentarily and then, with his brother who was with him, quickly made an exit through the rear door.

There was immediate chaos as the major and his men pushed Quinn and the dentist aside; Shouting, the general's invading squad rushed into the hall and tried to open the door, but it held fast. Soldiers sprayed the lock with bullets, shredding the door, allowing the major to kick it down. The palace was rapidly and thoroughly searched; the president of South Vietnam and his brother had escaped.

At headquarters, Big Minh was furious as he screamed orders to a new troop of men and at the major who had failed his mission.

"You will find them, or else you will find yourselves among your ancestors before this night is over. Now go!" The men hurried out of the room, determined to follow Minh's orders, and save their own lives.

Quinn and the dentist remained standing in front of the general who was obviously anxious; most likely because he knew, that if the mission to find the president failed, his own life was in jeopardy. "You two wait here until those bastards have been caught!" The general poured himself a generous glass of whiskey; there was no offer for anyone join him.

Two hours passed in which Big Minh paced, drank, then stumbled to his desk to answer the phone. Quinn and the dentist dared not sit.

They shuffled while pondering their own fate until the sudden ringing of the phone startled them to attention.

"Where?" Minh, quite drunk, shouted into the phone as spittle spurted onto the receiver. "What! Is the bishop there? Well, keep everything as it is! I'll send the dentist and the doctor." The general slammed down the phone and shouted for his adjutant who rushed into the room. "Get these men into a jeep and take them to the cathedral!" Turning to Quinn and the dentist he cryptically said, "Do your duty." "Now, go!"

The jeep carrying Quinn and the dentist screeched to a halt in front of the cathedral; the most imposing edifice representing Catholic power in Vietnam. Entering through the great doors of the cathedral, Quinn saw a crowd of soldiers in front of the steps leading to the alter. As Quinn and the dentist approached, the major, who had apparently saved his reputation, gave an order for the soldiers to disperse.

Like a curtain parting, the soldiers gave way to reveal two bodies lying on the steps of the alter. Quinn recognized the president, positioned on his back, frozen in death with three bullets having struck him in the neck and chest, his blood running downward in rivulets from step to step until it pooled at the major's feet. The other body was mutilated beyond recognition; bullets had almost decapitated the brother leaving only a portion of his lower jaw intact.

Without faltering, the dentist went about his gruesome work, prying out teeth, first from the president, then from what was left of his brother; the products of murder were placed in small bags and labeled. Quinn stood motionless, gazing at was left of the semblance of democracy in his country: now, corrupt. The leadership of South Vietnam was murdered in a cathedral, apparently while claiming sanctuary. The portent of this act did not bode well for a country now in the hands of anarchy.

Quinn signed the required documents which had been thrust at him by the major. He then turned and walked slowly into the early morning light breaking upon Saigon; a capital whose residents would soon learn of the changes in store for them following the death of their president. Quinn was certain that his future would be doomed if he remained anywhere in Vietnam. If the new government, Big Minh, did not "take care of him," then the Americans surely might. It would not take any stretch of the imagination to link Lansman and his "company" with the doctor who witnessed the brutal change in regime.

Through his connections, Lansman was already aware of what had happened at the cathedral and the bedlam that had followed when Big Minh declared himself president; two days after which Minh was arrested and replaced by a triumvirate of generals also seeking power. When Quinn met with the colonel to brief him, his report was dismissed with the wave of a hand.

"I know what happened. It's a shit storm. They know about you, and worse, they know about me. I guarantee you that the three jokers now running this country are going to be after your scalp."

Quinn shook his head in disbelief. "But why, I had nothing to do with it? I only did what you asked of me, and what general Minh ordered me to do."

Lansman was sober and at his managerial best. "Yes, you did what everyone told you to do. Now, they're going to blame everyone, including you, who had anything to do with Big Minh, in order to save their own asses."

It took some courage, but Quinn spoke curtly with Lansman. "You have put me in this position. I have done everything you have asked me to do ever since you recruited me at the Rex Hotel, and I left the bicycle shop. I think you owe me some protection."

"Doctor Quinn, this has turned out to be more of a mess than any of us could have predicted. I have been ordered to leave Vietnam, and soon. You have been an invaluable source of information for me, and I will keep my promise to you; America always keeps its promises. Now that it's over, I'll help you find the friends you've been looking for. You and I are leaving tonight for Guam. Get your things together, and say goodbye to whomever you want, but under no circumstances are you to tell anyone where you're going."

Quinn smiled. At last. Perhaps, now, he would find Sal and René. As to saying goodbye, the only farewell he had to make was to his country, Vietnam; a land that he would never see again.

18

Three into Ten

All air traffic into Saigon had been held up due to a large number of arriving American troop transports. Plane after plane, landing in sequence, turned the once sleepy airport into a military hub and reception center unparalleled in its history. Quinn waited with Colonel Lansman on the tarmac watching as hundreds of American combat troops disembarked the massive C-130's.

Young men milled around joking with one another, surprised by the intensity of Vietnam's heat and humidity. For many of these soldiers, it was the first time they had ever left the United States; little did they know that the jungles of Vietnam would claim over 58,000 of them for its own.

Quinn could not help observing the faces of these young men. Their innocence and juvenile playfulness betrayed their apprehension of the horrors they would soon encounter.

Arrival of these troops was accompanied by the docking of ships carrying cargos containing the necessities of war, including helicopters and supplies essential to sustain an army preparing for the unknown.

These helicopters would fly seemingly endless hours of troop transport missions, combat patrols, and medical evacuation.

Saigon was ebullient. The arrival of the Americans in great numbers meant greater profits for a nation already entangled in corruption: it gave the corrupt an opportunity to sell the country to the highest bidder. Quinn would never see the results of the wholesale introduction of war for profit: he would leave his country and only remember the genesis of the turmoil that would eventually embroil it and explode.

Lansman kept checking with the transport terminal for a departure time as he had orders to report to the "company" headquarters in Washington, as soon as possible. His departure had been ordered on the heels of another presidential assassination: John Fitzgerald Kennedy. The turbulence and uncertainty in Vietnam were mirrored in the United States. The citizens of each country had no premonition of the events that would soon unfold both in the United States and in Southeast Asia. The American people knew nothing about Vietnam, let alone where it was located, and the Vietnamese had no idea of what the infusion of an American army meant for its country's future.

Lansman's plans for Quinn included rapid departure and, finally, disclosure of the information he had promised to Quinn regarding the location of his friends. Although he had provided Quinn with a choice of destinations, including Paris, Quinn only wanted to join his friends, perhaps the only people in the world that meant anything to him, wherever they were.

Surrounded by confusion and the crowds of military personnel, Quinn waited on the hot tarmac, trying to sort out his future. Returning to Paris was not a good option. In France, he would be shunned because he was a reminder of their government's failed colonial policy. In his homeland, he was a fugitive from the North and a suspect in the South because he had been trained by the French and recruited to collaborate with the American intelligence service. In reality, his options were limited; there was no other choice for him to make. He was a man without a country; a physician with no place to practice medicine.

Meanwhile, three thousand-five hundred miles to the east in the

Truk islands of Micronesia, Sal and René were settled into their new home and were making progress in establishing routine medical care for the Truk community. Their little hospital had changed the lives, and in some cases, saved the lives of these island natives. Since it had opened, a new wing to the hospital had been built and René had trained three women to become "nurses," an occupation that had increased their status within the community.

Each morning, Sal and René made their rounds, accompanied by the newly trained nurses. Clinic sessions during the day were frequently interrupted by delivering babies, a routine occurrence due to the high rate of pregnancies. René delivered many by herself as she was quite proficient; Sal would assist if there were complications, or if the delivery required forceps.

One delivery in particular gained the hospital much prestige among the islands. An expectant mother, a dwarf, as she was described, was brought to the hospital from a neighboring island in heavy labor, unable to deliver naturally because of her deformed pelvis. She had been in labor for sixteen hours.

"This is going to be a tough one," Sal mused, preoccupied with rapidly assessing the tiny person lying in front of him on the verge of convulsions. "We'd better set up for a caesarian," he told René, who quickly prepared the small operating room. After positioning the patient, she became the anesthetist, dripping the ether onto the cone covering the mother's nose and mouth.

As usual, heads peeked through the windows and doorway to watch the procedure with curiosity and fascination. Ordinarily, in a conventional setting, observers would be shuttered out, but on Truk, it was Sal and René's policy to let the islanders in on the secrets of medicine, thereby gaining their trust.

The pungent smell of ether made a great impression on the villagers as they watched Sal make an incision on the taut, pregnant belly, open it up, and quickly deliver a screaming baby to the delight of the onlookers. Sal closed the incision, René stopped the flow of ether, and the new mother revived as the baby was placed on the new mother's breast to suckle. Surely, this patient would have died prior to the arrival of the husband and wife medical team.

Sal and René were content with their new life in Truk beyond anything they could have imagined. With Kimeo's help, Sal and René became fluent in the Micronesian language to the delight of the islanders. Each month that passed free of strife on these serene islands validated their decision to live and practice medicine here. They had genuinely found joy in their work, and the native population's appreciation for Sal and René gave them a daily sense of satisfaction.

Sal's memories of Legion battles and subsequent imprisonment were relegated to a distant memory; they were no longer an obstacle to his progress and maturity, or his new life with René. René felt blessed that she could share, in totality, love and a life with Sal, her husband, lover, friend, and colleague. Sal and René had found their new home.

The hospital was thriving, and every day brought anticipation among the islanders of what new changes might be next. Medical supplies from France arrived on a regular schedule. On one occasion, a surprise: a generator was discovered in the shipment which facilitated nighttime emergency treatment in an operating room that was otherwise lit by kerosene lamps. The first-time artificial light was the source of tremendous joy and celebration by islanders who had never been witness to this modern convenience.

Meanwhile, in the Saigon evening, after the influx of military transports had slowed down, Quinn and Lansman were ready to board their plane when a Vietnamese military jeep unexpectedly came rushing onto the tarmac. It screeched to a halt directly in front of them. Quinn recognized the major that approached him as the adjutant who had worked for Big Minh.

"Dr. Quinn, I have come here to arrest you." The major seemed nervous and kept on looking at the driver of his jeep. Lansman immediately stepped in front of Quinn as if to shield him. "You must come with me now!" said the major.

"This man is under the protection of the United States," said Lansman. "You have no authority to arrest him. Do you understand?"

The major's breathing quickened, and he began to sweat profusely. "I have been ordered by the commanding generals who have assumed control of the government to arrest him. He must come." The major, thrusting the arrest warrant at Lansman, was surprised when the colonel took the documents and tore them apart, letting them flutter down to the major's feet.

"This man has been implicated in the murder of the president. The generals need him to answer for his crime."

Lansman laughed as he looked at the major who was on the verge of trembling. "I know who you are. You're the adjutant who put Minh in his grave. I know everything about you, and what happened. Your government wants a scapegoat, and if you don't get back into your Goddamn jeep, I'll give them one."

Visibly shaking, the major sputtered, "But what shall I tell them? I have been given orders."

"You tell them that you were too late, and that our flight had already departed. That's what you tell them. Then you pay off that piece of shit driver of yours. Am I clear?"

Quinn said nothing. He had been apprehensive all along that his good fortune would not last. Nothing that had ever benefited him, had ever endured. As he witnessed the exchange between the major and Lansman, he a visualized Vietnamese soldiers tearing him away from the plane that would carry him to freedom. There were no soldiers. The major picked up the pieces of the warrant and crept back to his jeep, whispering something to his driver. Lansman kept his eyes on the jeep as it disappeared through the gates of the airport. He and Quinn were shortly thereafter called to board their plane. Lansman continued as he climbed the steps. "Pieces of shit. This whole country is a piece of shit."

"Thank you," was all Quinn could muster.

"Bullshit. It's the least I could do. You're a good guy, doctor, and you deserve a life."

As they settled into their seats, Quinn was curious about what Lansman would do next.

"What will you do, now, colonel?"

"Me? I'll go back to Washington. Tell them what a crap situation it is here; But they won't listen. Look at all these troops arriving; Washington has already made up its mind."

"Perhaps, when you give them your full appraisal, you can change some minds."

"Let me tell you something, Dr. Quinn. Sometimes, Americans jump before they look. We are well-intentioned, but don't always see things through the eyes of others. Can you understand that?"

"I'm sorry for your people," Quinn replied absently. As he looked around the airport through his window, he knew that Lansman was right.

All of the troops and equipment scattered around the airstrip spoke to an American commitment in Vietnam. The Americans would be sorry, as much as the French had been; they had no idea what they were up against. He had witnessed, and experienced, the chaos from north to south, and the dedication of the North to convert the South. Now, the North would be equally devoted to the destruction of the Americans.

As the transport plane reached altitude, Quinn looked out of the window, staring at the country to which he would never return. The plumes of smoke in the north: confirmed to Quinn that the struggle for the country had begun. The smoke arose from bombardments and overt military action from a well-concealed enemy. Arrival of the Americans had initiated battles that would rage for years to come. Quinn turned away from the window and let the drone of the plane's engines lull him into a restless sleep.

Lansman sitting opposite was lost in his own thoughts on strategies to convince his superiors of their futile efforts to support South Vietnam. It was a burden that he would carry for the rest of his life. In Washington, Lansman would be a solitary voice crying in the wilderness of ignorance and folly.

As he watched Quinn, he realized that the doctor represented the last of a people who would escape from the torment and carnage that was to come. If convincing Americans was to be in vain, he would at least keep his promise to the man who had done all that was asked of him to help him keep Vietnam from descending into madness. Lansman would put Quinn on the ferry in Guam scheduled to carry medical supplies from

Guam to Truk and re-unite him with the only people who had ever meant anything to him- Sal and René.

The intelligence chief and the physician parted company on the pier at Guam. As Quinn made his way up the ferry's gangway, he turned to see Lansman get into a black government sedan. He rolled down the window and gave Quinn a final salute.

Lansman had kept his promise: Quinn was on his way to Truk.

On the short three-day voyage, a myriad of thoughts besieged Quinn as he paced the deck of the supply ferry. Utmost, of course, was the question of whether Sal was still there. What if Lansman's information was not current? How would he find Sal? These and other questions haunted Quinn as traveled south to a foreign destination, and an unknown future.

The arrival of medical supplies from Guam was always a festive occasion for the Truk Lagoon; it was a holiday to be celebrated by all who waited on the dock, excited to see what would arrive on the island. Generators, equipment for another radio station, and a water purification system had all made the lives of the islanders easier; for Sal and René these were necessities imperative to assure that their hospital would survive.

Excitement on the dock mounted as the supply ferry came into view between two of the islands. Sal and René stood in the brightness and heat of the day surrounded by their island "family," who began to sing the same song they had sung when they had first arrived. The ship's whistle answered, to the delight of those waiting.

On the bow stood Quinn, shielding his eyes in order to see the island where he could possibly spend the rest of his life. Lansman had made no other arrangements for Quinn; no one on the island knew that he was arriving.

As the ship neared the dock, Quinn gulped in astonishment when he saw the two white people craning their necks to see what was on board.

Instantly, he saw Sal, dressed in a fading scrub top with his arms around a woman he recognized- the kindest woman he had ever known. It was René. Quinn suppressed his impulse to shout or wave. He wanted to savor the sight of the two people whose memory he had kept alive through all the years of separation and anguish; he began to sob visibly as a wave of relief overwhelmed him.

Sal had gained weight, no longer the frail prisoner that Quinn had nursed back to health. René, slim and tanned, was as beautiful as he remembered last seeing her on the day he left Paris. It was clear that the people who surrounded them, singing and swaying, were a part of their lives.

Sal looked up at the bow and saw the figure whose gaze was transfixed on him; then he saw the tears streaming down a face that he recognized instantly. "Oh, my God!" He stepped forward and pointed to show René. She let out a gasp, "It can't be." Sal began to shout as he ran to the ship that had cast lines to be made fast. "Quinn, Quinn, is it you?" René followed, waving madly with, "Quinn, it's us!" Quinn grasped the railing with both hands; he was visibly shaken and thought that he would faint. "I know," he murmured unable to raise his voice because of his sobbing. "I know, it is you! Both of you are here! We are…" He was looking straight down at them from the bow, not believing his good fortune, all of his doubts and questions vanishing.

Sal, with René trailing behind him, ran to the gangway that was barely in place as they both jumped on the ramp that would lead them to their friend. Quinn met them before they even reached the deck. Sal beamed as Quinn raced into his arms and René completed the threesome's embrace.

The villagers on the dock were not perplexed or astonished. They knew that if Sal and René demonstrated such affection for the stranger, he must be someone very special. The ship's horn gave out a final blast. The three of them, Sal, René, and Quinn, could finally put ten years of suffering and hard work behind them. Together again, they could now look forward to a future among friends, safe and at peace, on an island in the middle of the Pacific Ocean blessed by the sun.

THE END

CPSIA information can be obtained
at www.ICGtesting.com
Printed in the USA
BVHW081420130820
586217BV00003B/106